Too Many Losing Heroines!

"I *knew* it!
She's after his chastity,
that witch!"
Yanami
Anna

"I wonder if he likes smart girls better…"
Yakishio Lemon

Komari
Chika
"H-he called me…
The president…
called me cute."

"I'm very proud of you, Oniisama. That's my big brother."
Nukumizu Kaju

LOSERS
ON THE BEACH
STAR

~SUN, SURF, AND SINKING SHIPS~
PENGINICE
PENGINICE

CONTENTS

Too Many Losing Heroines!

NOVEL

1

WRITTEN BY
Takibi Amamori

ILLUSTRATED BY
Imigimuru

Airship

Seven Seas Entertainment

MAKE HEROINE GA OSUGIRU! Vol. 1
by Takibi AMAMORI

Seven Seas press and purchase enquiries can be sent to Marketing Manager Lauren Hill at press@gomanga.com. Information regarding the distribution and purchase of digital editions is available from Digital Manager CK Russell at digital@gomanga.com.

Follow Seven Seas Entertainment online at sevenseasentertainment.com.

TRANSLATION: Matthew Jackson
COVER DESIGN: H. Qi
INTERIOR LAYOUT & DESIGN: Clay Gardner
COPY EDITOR: Jade Gardner
PROOFREADER: Catherine Pedigo
EDITOR: Callum May
PREPRESS TECHNICIAN: Melanie Ujimori, Jules Valera
MANAGING EDITOR: Alyssa Scavetta
EDITOR-IN-CHIEF: Julie Davis
PUBLISHER: Lianne Sentar
VICE PRESIDENT: Adam Arnold
PRESIDENT: Jason DeAngelis

ISBN: 979-8-89160-307-3
Printed in Canada
First Printing: August 2024
10 9 8 7 6 5 4 3 2 1

CHARACTERS

LOSERS AND FRIENDS

Nukumizu Kazuhiko
First-year. Proud loner.

Yanami Anna
First-year. Happy and hungry.

Komari Chika
First-year. Lit club. A bit far gone.

Yakishio Lemon
First-year. Fastest & loudest girl on the track team.

Nukumizu Kaju
Second-year, junior high. Little sister from heaven.

Tsukinoki Koto
Third-year. Vice president of the lit club.

Shikiya Yumeko
Second-year. Student council. Most fashionable zombie.

Tamaki Shintarou
Third-year. President of the lit club.

Amanatsu Konami
Social studies teacher. Class 1-C's very own.

Konuki Sayo
School nurse. Old classmates with Amanatsu.

FRIDAY. JUST TEN DAYS AWAY FROM SUMMER vacation. We'd survived the flames of semester finals, and I was celebrating by minding my own business at a special dive, very far away from school. I ordered my usual: large fries and a cup for the self-serve drink bar. I wiped the sweat from my brow and surveyed my surroundings. Couldn't act too suspicious. I waited for my fries before heading over to fill my cup.

"Let's do this."

The coast was clear. Not a single uniform from my school in sight. I reached into my bag and ruffled around for today's objective—the latest volume of *I Can Act Spoiled If My Little Sister Is Older than Me, Right?*

Soda in one hand, light novel in the other, and a big ol' pile of french fries. Oh yeah. Party time.

Too Many Losing Heroines!

LOSS 1

The Pro Childhood Friend Strikes Out

"I'M SO PROUD OF YOU, ONIICHAN. I KNOW, BABY. I KNOW how hard you work. You just let me take care of you, all right? You deserve to be pampered."

I sniffled. What a saint Kurumi-chan was. What a perfect little sister, the way she loved and cared for her big brother. These affirmation scenes could go on for up to twenty pages, and no, they never got old.

I shut the book and admired the heroine on the cover, wondering about when it would be my turn to love. When it would be my turn to have a pair of thighs to rest my weary head on.

"What's your problem, Sousuke?! Are you just not gonna do anything?!"

A shout from the neighboring table took me out of my reverie. Someone was having a bit of a lover's spat. It was always something with these people. Maybe it was an extrovert thing. Whatever it was, they needed Kashitani Kurumi to set them straight. They didn't call her "the Sweetest Angel" for nothin'.

None of my business. I started to get up to grab some melon soda (so as to properly enjoy the following insert illustration) but quickly sat my butt back down.

I'd goofed bad. Real bad. That couple? They were wearing the same school uniform as me. As if that wasn't bad enough, I *recognized* them. We were *classmates*.

The one who'd shouted was Yanami Anna—one of those bubbly types. Popular. Sitting across from her was Hakamada Sousuke. Again, popular. Handsome. Didn't know they were dating, but I wasn't exactly surprised. They were glued at the hip around school. The question remained: Why had they picked *here*, my family restaurant hangout, to have their falling out?

I returned to my book, half focused on listening in.

"Unless you go stop her *right now*, Karen-chan's gonna be gone forever. You realize that, don't you? Do you have any idea how far away Britain is?"

"We said our goodbyes," the guy protested.

"And you honestly mean to tell me you took her seriously?!"

Boy, talk about trite. Where had I heard all that before? It really was odd finishing up my story while another was unraveling literally right next to me.

"Karen" sounded familiar. I recalled that we'd had a transfer student come in not too long ago. Himemiya Karen. She was a real whirlwind. The first thing out of her mouth was an accusation. Apparently, Hakamada had groped her or something, I dunno.

Wait, she's going back already? No pacing, I swear.

"Should I not have?" Hakamada asked.

"You wouldn't get it. You don't know how it feels to be in..." Yanami hung her head and bit her lip.

"Anna, I—"

"Forget it," she said quietly. She looked up, composed, and dropped a bike key on the table. "Go. She's waiting for you."

"You're sure?"

"She's a patient girl. Just don't keep her long. Make her happy—she deserves it."

"Thanks, Anna. I won't screw it up this time."

Yanami nodded. "I know you won't. Don't forget I've got a shoulder to lend if she ends up dumping you on your butt."

"I'm..." A moment later, and he was gone. Without so much as a second glance back at his friend.

Yanami stood there for a while before plopping back down lifelessly. "Yeah. You better not finish that sentence," she muttered.

And there I was. Just kinda sitting there. A foreigner in an exotic land of drama and social lives. I decided the best thing I could do for her dignity was to simply pretend I wasn't there. So I did exactly that and hid behind the menu.

Until...

Bro, she wouldn't.

Yanami Anna, fresh off the rejection bus, reached for a glass. The glass of the man who had just ripped her heart out.

Don't. Do not. No! my soul cried in vain.

She held the glass tenderly in both hands, and then, ever so slowly, in the straw went between her lips. Line: officially crossed.

Her eyes wandered this way, that way, before finally landing on mine. Yikes. Uh-oh. Bad. Various other exclamations of displeasure.

Part of me prayed she wouldn't recognize me. This hope was dashed as soon as I saw the red start to creep up her cheeks. And then—coffee. Coffee spraying from her lips. Coffee on the table. Coffee everywhere. She spat out the drink, and what didn't come out she choked on.

This, friends, was why I preferred the two-dimensional.

My only recourse was to double down. I had seen nothing. You could tell by how good I was at whistling and how invested I was in the menu. Unfortunately, my talents were wasted on the likes of Yanami, who marched right on over and sat across from me. Because God forbid we both minded our own business.

"You. I know you. You're Nukumizu-kun. We're in the same class," she accused.

"O-oh, well, if it isn't Yanami-san," I sputtered. "What a coinkydink."

I wasn't convincing anyone. Certainly not Yanami. The blush climbed up to her ears. She shot me her most serious, intimidating look.

"Th-this better stay between us!"

"Sure, uh, yeah. Didn't see anything anyway. Not me."

"That's right! Not a thing!" She shot up out of her seat, awkwardly avoiding eye contact.

In my defense, I'd gotten here first. Anything I had happened to bear witness to was not my responsibility.

Whatever. It was done. I put it out of my mind and headed to the drink bar. A nice cold melon soda would cool my head.

When I got back, though, Yanami was still standing there at my table. She had her wallet open, clumsily counting coins—yeah, she was clearly broke. I went to slip by her, but my conscience held me back. There was no real tactful way out of this situation with her loitering right where I needed to be.

This was for the good of my free time, which she was currently wasting. That was all there was to it. I counted to ten in my head, then called out to her. "You, uh...need some help?"

"Wha?" she croaked, halfway to crying. She nodded slowly.

I took her receipt. How much could she have possibly eaten? The answer: a lot. Hakamada had ordered a friggin' steak combo. Yanami, bless her heart, had made an attempt to settle for soup and salad, only to give up and order a burger *and* dessert. The lack of foresight on display here was truly impressive.

"All right, well, I'll cover you today," I said. "Just pay me back Monday."

There went my evening plans to go light novel shopping. A sacrifice, to be sure, but eh. As much as I would have liked to, I couldn't just leave a classmate out to dry, especially not after what she'd just been through.

"Really? You're sure? I mean, I hardly know you," she said.

Hey, whatever gets you gone faster—aaand she's sitting down.

"Are you, uh, not leaving?" I asked.

"Thanks, Nukumizu-kun. I really appreciate it. Guess I had you all wrong."

Ah, yes, insult me while you're at it. I was beginning to regret giving in to empathy.

"Not leaving? No?"

Yanami folded her hands together and stared off into the distance. Quite irreverently. "We're childhood friends, you know."

Oh, do tell.

She did. "When we were kids, Sousuke made me a ring out of clovers, and he asked me to marry him. Can you believe it?"

Tears welled in her eyes and quickly spilled over.

"Wh-whoa, hey!" I blubbered. "Are you good?"

This was going well, if you ignored all the prying eyes and literally everything else about the situation. I fled to the drink bar again, picked a tea bag at random, and plunked it in some water for her.

"Here, just..." I came back and handed it to her. "Collect yourself."

"Thanks." She took a sip. "Mh, I like this."

"Good. I think that's rose hip." I remembered the label or whatever that I'd read while I was over there. "It's good for your skin."

Yanami cast her eyes down. "Not like I have anyone *to* look good for anymore."

This was just plain painful. I racked my brain for literally anything to say to get us off the subject and her out of my hair. Wasted effort.

"One large fry!" a newcomer in a uniform called out.

"I'm sorry?" I blinked. Suddenly there were fries. And it was on my bill. "I'm sorry, we didn't—"

"I care about Karen-chan a lot. I do. She's a dear friend to me," Yanami continued. "It's just, well... She just *showed up*, you know? It's like, were Sousuke and I just not together for over a decade? What happened to all that?"

She blew her nose into a napkin, then went straight for the fries.

"Hey, did you order these?"

"*I'm* the one he asked to marry. How is that fair? How can he just lie like that?"

I could think of a few things that were less than fair in that moment. Welp, I'd made my bed. I could either keep whining or suck it up and lie in it.

"How old were you when he made that promise?" I asked, barely holding back a sigh.

"Before elementary school, so like, four or five?" she replied.

Yeah, nah. Not legally binding.

Another fry. "Do you think that counts as cheating? It has to, right? Like, how do you just jump ship like that after *one* transfer student with a couple honkers shows up?"

Now that was an interesting angle. I hadn't pegged Hakamada as a philanderer. Himemiya Karen was a looker—no one could argue that—but Yanami had her charms for sure. Unfortunately for her, however, she hadn't been born with that X factor that all the anime and manga title girls had. I genuinely felt for her in that respect.

"I didn't know you guys were actually dating," I said.

"Huh? O-oh, no. I mean, did it look like we were?" Yanami blushed and giggled to herself. "People always did say we were super cute together. Can't blame you for assuming."

I blinked at her. "So you're *not* dating. Then literally how is it cheating?"

Yanami winced. "W-well, you said so yourself! We *kind of* were! Sorta! We *would have* been if it weren't for that home-wrecker and her mommy milkers!"

The best of friends, those two sounded.

"Also!" she coped. "Who knows? Maybe he'll change his mind at the last minute or something."

"I'm sorry to say the eleventh hour has passed."

Yeah, I was a bit of an expert. I'd read my fair share of rom-coms, and her goose was downright cooked. I sipped my melon soda. With reverence.

"You wanna know something?" Yanami asked. "Just between you and me, Sousuke and I have bathed together."

"Uh-huh. When you were four or five?"

Sousuke and his new girl would hit that base in no time.

"Okay, but our families are close! We practically have their blessing already! That's, like, one of the most important parts about having a wed...ding." The tears returned with a vengeance.

"Sh-should I be concerned?"

"The wedding..." Yanami whined. "I had a dress picked out and everything. And that tits-for-brains stole it from me..."

Oof, that one was on her. You never picture the dress that far in advance, or your rival wearing it instead of you, for that matter. I wondered what the rejection bus's schedule looked like, because I was over this passenger.

"I know. I know, okay? It's my fault for sitting around for so long. I should have been brave," she said.

"You, uh, need a refill? The mint tea here's pretty good."

"No... Tastes like toothpaste." Yanami pouted, then smiled. She wiped her eyes clean. "Sorry. Bit much, huh?"

"Hey, no worries," I said. That wasn't the apology I was personally waiting for.

"I'll be okay. As long as Sousuke's happy, I can settle for best friends."

"Y-yeah. Okay."

Yanami was a roller coaster of emotion. She went on and on, and I just sat there eating french fries. Listening. Doing my best to be as patient as possible. There was a word for heroines like her whose ships wound up lost at sea.

They were the losers.

Yanami Anna was a losing heroine.

***

Three days went by. It was Monday now, back at school. I leaned back up from the faucet, shut off the water, and wiped my mouth. City water was never any good, although that depended on who you asked. Granted, most didn't know what I knew. Most were blind to the fact that water could, in fact, taste different from tap to tap, even within the same building. I, Nukumizu Kazuhiko of Tsuwabuki High School's class 1-C, fancied myself one of the enlightened few.

"Now that's the stuff," I muttered.

It was just before fourth period. The first-floor sink in front of the library in that new annex was my current sanctuary. Early in the morning, this was the place to be for top shelf tap water. Being further from the rooftop water tank meant the chlorine levels were minimal, and you didn't want any of that swimming in your stomach right before lunch.

My thirst quenched, I started on my way back to class, calculating in my head the perfect pace. Arrive too early, and there'd doubtless be a conversation happening right at my desk, and I wasn't about to deal with that. A leisurely stroll would get me there just in time.

I thought back to last week—to Yanami Anna. The boys had made quite a fuss over her on the first day of school. She was pretty, I gave her that, but it was clear to me from the get-go that we lived in different worlds. I was content occupying mine and she occupying hers. Apparently, though, as evidenced by recent events, that understanding didn't run both ways. I genuinely couldn't remember the last time I'd spoken with a girl for that long. She showed me flashes of charm, and she showed me flashes of insanity. I couldn't make heads or tails of her.

But that was all in the past. Once I got my money back, that would be the end of it. I'd go back to my world, and she'd go back to hers, and I'd look back and think, "Yep, that sure was a thing that happened."

I checked my watch as I slid open the classroom door. Thirty seconds to the bell—perfect.

I clicked my tongue. Not perfect. Yakishio Lemon of all people was sitting on my desk, that happy-go-lucky, tan girl on the track team. We'd come from the same junior high. She was literally always smiling, always talking with someone. She was magnetic. And she wouldn't budge an inch until the bell sounded.

Taking the long way around the room, I slipped by my currently-colonized desk and reached into my pocket for the old receipt I kept specifically for times like these. In the time it took me to toss the thing, the bell rang. I made my way back, assured of my victory.

No one moved. The invaders remained. I glanced at the chalkboard. "4th period—World History, 10 minutes late, self-study," it read.

I had miscalculated. None of these people were going to study. They'd just gotten an extra ten minutes added to their break. I wandered over to the notice board, wiping away the nervous sweat on my brow.

Wow, an inter-high rally? Boy howdy, and the archery club had made nationals for the third year in a row. I was so incredibly invested in this information. With enthusiastically feigned interest, I scanned the schedule for that rally thing: opening ceremony, July 22nd. Girls volleyball, 22nd to the 25th. Canoeing, 28th to 31st.

"We should totally do lunch together!"

I knew that shrill, immersion-breaking voice anywhere. It was Himemiya Karen. I snuck a peek and, to little surprise, saw Hakamada and Yanami with her. Honestly, though, I could feel the main heroine vibes from here. She had the looks, the presence, the...personalities.

Yanami had on her best smile. That was the biggest surprise. I'd expected, well...I wasn't sure what I expected. Different worlds. Maybe in hers, relationships coming and going was the norm.

"I'm good." Yanami kept smiling. "Don't wanna be a third wheel or anything."

"Don't be like that," the transfer student argued. "We're still friends, you know?"

"That's right," Hakamada agreed. "You don't have to try and be considerate. I see right through you."

Yanami gave him an awkward elbow poke. "Speak for yourself. I'm trying to do you a favor here, bud."

"Anna..." Himemiya Karen sighed.

"Yeah?" Before Yanami could get her next few words out, Himemiya threw her arms around her. "C-come on, now, Karen-chan. What's all this for?"

"Thank you. You're my best friend in the whole world," said tits-for-brains (not my words).

"Come on, people are staring." She patted her dear friend on the shoulder.

Evidently, I'd been worried for nothing. Yanami seemed pretty much over it—at a glance. That was when I noticed her legs trembling and her fists clenched white behind Himemiya's back. Oh, she was over it. In an entirely different sense entirely.

"So, lunch," Himemiya pressed. "How about we—"

"E-excuse me." Just as I was starting to see steam billowing out of Yanami's ears, I cut in. "Yanami-san?"

All three pairs of eyes centered on me. This, right here, was exactly what I was talking about with different worlds. Oh, the sin I had committed—the absolute *travesty* it was for the background character to butt into the main plot.

By some miracle, I managed to keep myself composed and my voice from cracking. "You're on duty today, right? Amanatsu-sensei wants your help in the printing room."

"Oh." Yanami slipped away from her prison. "Yeah, sure. I'll be right there. Thanks." She made for the door but turned around just before leaving the classroom. "You know what? I could actually use a hand."

***

There I was, next to Yanami-san, walking down the hallway together. What was I even supposed to say? I glanced at her.

Yanami Anna. She was certainly pretty. Fluffy, flowing hair. Big, round eyes. Gentle features. I could see why she was so popular with the guys. Like, let's just get it out there. This girl had the *looks.* Hakamada. My man. *This girl* was your best friend for over a decade? What were you thinking, passing her up? Sure, Himemiya Karen was potentially prettier, had bigger personalities, more grace...

"Whatcha starin' at?" Yanami leaned over and peered at me.

"N-noth—uh, nothing," I stammered, tearing my eyes from her face. Those thoughts were best kept to myself.

"So tell me," she whispered real low, stepping in close. I swear she knew what she was doing. "Was that little act back there just for me?"

"I-it looked like you needed a hand. Sorry if I was butting in or whatever."

"Nah. Thanks. I was straight up about to rip those udders clean off her chest." She didn't even blink as she said this. "Where are we going, anyway? The teacher doesn't actually want me, I assume."

"Only one reason Amanatsu-sensei would put us on self-study," I said. "She forgot the printouts again. Might as well help her before all hell breaks loose."

Amanatsu Konami was our homeroom and social studies teacher, and she was a chronic truant. Not on purpose, mind you. She just had a bad habit of mixing up the class schedule, forgetting her materials, walking into the wrong class, and she probably had trouble remembering to breathe too. Generally, self-study meant she had forgotten her materials.

I opened the door to the printing room, entirely unsurprised to find Amanatsu-sensei, yet somewhat surprised at the state she was in.

"Er, is everything okay?" I asked.

It was like a paper factory had exploded in there. Papers littered the floor, the table, and of course covered the printer with which Amanatsu-sensei was presently doing battle. She was a minuscule creature, easily mistaken for a student were she in uniform. And a creature she was.

"Ah, Yanami!" she said. "You should be in class, you kn*wakh*!"

Amanatsu-sensei slipped on one of the papers on the floor, and down she went, flat on her face, sending yet more papers flying. Some called her clumsy. I called her a walking safety hazard.

"Thought you could maybe use some help," said Yanami.

"Right you are! Be a pal and get me enough copies for the class, wouldja?"

We knelt down and started examining the paper carpet at our feet. Which sheets were we meant to be copying? Only God knew. The allotted ten-minute self-study time had come and gone by the time the three of us managed to fish out the right papers.

"I really nailed today's lesson too. It's gonna knock your socks off," Amanatsu-sensei said proudly.

To her credit, she did put a lot of effort into her lesson plans. I took a peek at one of the copies.

"Sensei, we haven't covered this material," I said. "I thought we were doing Chinese history today."

"Look, bub, I dunno who you are, but you must have a few screws loose," she ranted. "Second-years cover the Byzantine Empire in July, and don't you forget it. Which you won't once you learn just how moe those guys were."

"Ma'am, you're teaching class 1-C." Which happened to be mine, fun fact.

"I'm *what*?!" All our work fluttered to the floor once again. "I can save this! We've still got forty minutes. That's plenty of time to get a lesson together!"

Maybe not enough to have *the lesson,* I thought.

Amanatsu-sensei flew from the printing room (but not before face-planting one more time). A real piece of art, that pedagogue.

The chaos settled, leaving us in its wake.

"Guess we should start cleaning."

"Probably," Yanami said. "She's never gonna get a new act, is she?"

We got to tidying up, and the silence quickly became awkward. What did boys typically say to girls when they were alone together in a printing room? I wasn't sure, but I did remember something important.

I cleared my throat. "So, uh, about the money I lent you Friday."

"Oh, duh! I don't actually have my wallet on me right now. Can you meet me at the old annex during lunch?" Yanami asked. "The fire escape stairs on the side."

"Huh? Uh, sure, I guess. Long as I get my money." She probably didn't want her friends in class catching her with a dork like me—or the guy who friend-zoned her, come to think of it.

I picked the papers back up, completely unfazed by the implications, and handed them to Yanami. She tapped them upright against the table, straightening the stack.

"You've probably noticed that they're dating now," she said quietly, eyes like a dead fish. She continued tapping the papers against the table.

"Sorta, I guess," I admitted. "I think you got those papers straight, by the way."

"Did you hear them inviting me to lunch? Wonder what that's about." The papers crinkled in her grip. "What if they're doing it on purpose? Trying to show off?" *Scrunch.*

"I mean, I only know him from group work, but he seems like a decent guy to me. I don't think he'd do that, do you?"

"No," she said. "No, you're right. Sousuke wouldn't do that."

"We're in agreement."

"He's an angel. Always has been. You should see his baby photos." Yanami shut her eyes, seemingly departing planet Earth. "You can tell. It's like he came straight from heaven. Oh, I just wanna post them online and watch the likes roll in!"

A good while passed while she giggled and reminisced to herself. After dawn, however, comes dusk.

"I get it now." Flames flickered in her eyes, dark and foreboding. "It's all *her* fault. *She's* the problem."

"I'm sorry?"

"Karen-chan's trying to break me, squash me, stifle me, keep me down so I won't touch *her* man," she raved.

"Let's take Hanlon's razor to this, shall we?"

"And here I thought we were friends. Sousuke's just under her spell. Yeah. That's it. That little witch seduced him." I recalled a time when Yanami had called Himemiya her "dear friend." "There's evil in those sandbags. Dark and pure and twisted evil. Tell me you're with me, Nukumizu-kun."

Personally, I sensed only hopes and dreams in them, but admitting that would have gotten me killed. I glanced at the door, praying to every god that my one way out would return. Moments later, the door miraculously flew open.

"Oh, thank god, you're—"

"Viva Byzantium!" Amanatsu-sensei shrieked. Immediate red flags.

"What are you talking about?"

"Turns out I didn't have jack for the first-years, so I was gonna just hide in the staff room until class was over. But *then*!" She had on the most smug grin. Society was doomed if these were the inheritors. "I was like, hey, why don't I just enlighten the youngins? Come on, we've got Byzantine moe to proselytize!"

"Ma'am, please remember this is a school, not a church," I said. I mean, I *had* prayed for this.

"Hey, I do my job just fine for the second-years."

"What if you, I dunno, brought a textbook and taught from that?" I proposed. "That can't be too hard. I believe in you."

"Ehhh, but I haven't prepared anything," Amanatsu-sensei whined.

"Improvise."

Somehow, my half-assed attempts at a pep talk worked. Amanatsu-sensei clenched her fist tight. "Yeah. Yeah! I'm a teacher! A teacher without a textbook."

"We will get you a textbook."

"D'aww, shucks. You're a good kid. But you should really get to class, though. Your teacher's probably wonderin' where you ran off to."

"You are my teacher, ma'am."

I was starting to run dangerously low on quips.

***

That afternoon, I made my way to our meeting spot and took a seat on the fire escape stairs outside. The place felt foreign to me. It was empty, secluded away from prying eyes—a private oasis. My fascination with tap water was, in truth, beginning to wane after four months of using it as my getaway this semester. This would make a good secondary escape.

I started to grab some bread to kill time until Yanami deigned to show up.

"Nukumizu-kun. There you are."

Yanami came trotting down the stairs. I looked up at her and was met with a face full of bare thigh.

"S-sorry!" I stammered. "I wasn't, er—"

"Please, God, save me." She plopped down. "Karen-chan just invited us to karaoke after school."

Ah, karaoke. The extroverts' art. That one such as her would seek *my* aid, well, a truly perilous art it must have been indeed.

"Uh, then go," I said.

Yanami held her head in her hands and made a sound like a dying goat. "And listen to those two sing a friggin' *duet* together?! I'd literally rather hurl myself off a bridge. Is that what you want?"

"Look, I've never been to karaoke." What in the world did she want me to do about it? "I'm not an expert in what that entails."

"Oh." She frowned suddenly and got real quiet. "Oh. Wow, um... Sorry, I-I didn't realize... Wow, I am so sorry. I don't even... Forget I said anything."

After all that? Seriously? Like, why, though? Was that necessary? Was my suffering really necessary?

"Can we just drop it, please? So about the money," I said.

"They keep insisting that nothing's changed, and, like, how it's no big deal or whatever..."

Aaand she brought her lunch. Are we really doing this over food?

I sighed. "I guess just take their word for it. Now the money?"

"I only found out officially the night you spotted me the cash. That they started dating, I mean." She stabbed her chopsticks into some taro. Again. And again. "*Looong* time for them to have gotten up to something."

"Sure, you can make assumptions, but what if they were just busy?"

"Sousuke's sister messaged me. She said she couldn't get a hold of him. Wanted to know if he was with me. And, of course, he wasn't."

"Oh..."

I was in danger. I looked to my curry bread for support.

"Wonder what they were so busy doing. What do you think?" That taro was so unbelievably dead.

"M-maybe their phones ran out of battery? Happens all the time."

"That's true. I should have more faith, huh? Ha. As if I have any of that left."

What is actually happening right now?

Yanami hung her head for a while before finally looking back up. "Sorry. I'm rambling."

"Y-you're good. I don't mind listening, I guess."

"Thanks. You're the only one I can really talk about this with, Nukumizu-kun. My friends wouldn't get it, and I definitely can't dump on acquaintances, y'know?"

Ah. So I wasn't even at acquaintance level. Noted.

"Let's eat before the bell sneaks up on us," I said. Complaining and food were about all there was between us, it seemed.

Yanami made a tired smile. "True. Lunchtime, after all."

We ate in silence. I scarfed down my curry bread in no time before I let my eyes wander over to her. What a surreal sight. Me, eating lunch with a girl.

People of her status were surely used to the ebb and flow of relationships, of hookups and breakups. Yanami was a good-looking girl. She'd doled out her fair share of rejections before, I was sure. The roles were just reversed this time around, and she had to live with that. Rejection was a part of life.

Well, *her* life.

"You..." The words came out on their own. I had no idea where I was even going with this. "You're...popular. With the guys, I mean. Personally, I think you've, y'know, got a little more going for you... Than Himemiya-san, I mean."

Yanami blinked at me and made that same face from the classroom that I hated. It was like I'd called her out in front of a live studio audience or something.

"I'll...take that as a compliment?" she finally said.

"Sorry. Weird. Forget it." This right here was why you kept your head down, Kazuhiko.

I heard her stifle a giggle next to me. She made a funny smile. I looked away.

"The attempt was sweet. Guess I still had the wrong idea about you." She carried a less-mangled piece of taro to her mouth.

Whatever her idea of me had been, something told me it wasn't charitable.

"Anyway," I said, "can I have that money now? This is the receipt."

"Sure. Thanks again for that, by the way." She suddenly froze. "Wait."

"Something wrong?"

"What's with that number? Am I crazy?"

"Well, you ordered that watermelon pancake right at the end. With ice cream."

"Okay." She nodded.

"And then you threw in the pork shabu-shabu udon salad on top of it."

"Salad's low cal," she added. Honestly, I admired the inhuman amount of trust she was placing in the word "salad" to hold that word salad of a dish together.

After what felt like forever, it seemed like I was finally going to get that money back. Yanami stared at the receipt, then at my outstretched hand, and then back at the receipt.

She nodded to herself. "So, just an idea, but what's your take on bartering?"

"Bartering?" I parroted. My interest was piqued.

Yanami blushed, fidgeted, and poked at some of the meat in her bento box with her chopsticks. "I-I could... Not that I'm all that amazing at it or anything, but, well, I'm short on cash, *sooo*... And Sousuke always liked when I did it for him."

"Okay?"

Where was she going with this? I followed her chopsticks down to the moist, supple chicken she was mercilessly toying with. Moist, supple meat. A blushing Yanami...

Wait, I thought. *Wait, no way! Is she implying what I think she's implying?!*

I shook my head at mach speed. "Wh-wh-what are you talking about?! We're in broad daylight! And at school!"

"I know I'm not the best cook, but I can manage an extra bento maybe," Yanami continued.

"A what now? A bento?"

"Uh, yeah?" She cocked her head to the side, completely oblivious. "What'd you think I said?"

"Nothing! Gotcha! Bento lunch!" I dug and scraped my mind back out of the gutter, then checked the receipt again. "I dunno if one's gonna cover all this, though."

I was rather proud of the nest egg I'd scrimped and saved up.

"Yeah, so what you can do is set a price for whatever I make you, and I'll keep doing it until the whole tab's covered."

Homemade lunch from a girl was definitely valuable. Perhaps even priceless to someone like me. This may have been my only chance at getting to experience such a luxury. The money I'd save on food would add up too.

On the other hand, oh god. Did I really want to keep skulking around behind people's backs just to play bento appraiser?

"Maybe we should—"

"I'll be back tomorrow. Same spot," Yanami interrupted. "Don't forget!"

She grinned from ear to ear, stuffed her face with yet more chicken, and I didn't have it in me to spoil her mood.

"Yep."

***

The first bell chimed, sounding the end of lunch. I sank into my chair as exhaustion crashed over me like a wave. How had a simple monetary transaction gotten so out of hand? And I still didn't have my money. We were going to "barter," apparently. Instead of cold, hard cash, I'd be paid in Yanami's homemade cooking.

Homemade cooking. Just for me. It still didn't feel real. I had to be dreaming.

I was resolute in one thing: We were midway through July, and I was gonna keep my head down for the rest of it. None would perceive me the remainder of this semester. This, I manifested in my mind's eye, and thus I was free from social interaction for the rest of the day. The technique had never failed me before.

"E-ex...excuse me. N-Nukumizu-kun?" The technique had failed me. A girl stood next to my desk and was making an extraordinarily valiant effort to speak words. "I-I'm…first-year. L-literature club!"

The girl choked on her own tongue and started to cough. I didn't know what she wanted, but I doubted she'd find it with me.

"Who from what?"

"K-Komari!" she spat. "From the literature club! Komari Chika!" Komari clung to the hem of her long, baggy summer button-up. She stared at me through teary eyes. "I-I need to…talk to you."

"About what? What do I have to do with your club?"

"Y-y-you're in it!"

"Say what?"

"What?"

Silence. I searched my memory and recalled a few months back, right after the entrance ceremony. I remembered taking a tour of the lit club and writing my name down on…something. On reflection, it must've been a sign-up form.

"You know, maybe I am," I said.

Komari Chika puffed a little sigh, then started mashing on her phone keyboard. When finished, she pointed the screen at me. It read, "The student council issued a warning to us about inactive members. We're already low as is."

Didn't take much detective work to figure out who the inactive member was.

More typing. "Be there after school, please."

"S-sure. I'll be there," I said.

It all came back to me. The lit club was all girls, except for the president. I'd felt too awkward to keep going, which was why

I stopped. If the representative they'd sent to round me up was any indication of the culture there, I had a feeling I'd made the right call.

***

I stood deep in the west annex, contemplating my life choices and regretting them immensely. All I wanted was to be home.

"Guessing this is the place."

Against my better judgment, I marched toward the club room door. It wasn't my favorite way to spend my afternoon, but they were low on members. Deep down, I empathized with my fellow underdogs. I couldn't bring myself to turn away, so I took a breath and reached for the doorknob.

"Oh. It's locked."

Time to go home. I had tried, and that was good enough for me.

I whipped around to find a phone screen in my face. "I have the key. Move," it read.

Komari Chika squeezed by me and unlocked the door. It would have been so much easier if she just used her words.

I followed her inside. Komari made a beeline for a chair, grabbed a book, and that was all from her. Usually, the rude types were supposed to come with soft sides. You know, to actually make them likable. This one was clearly defective.

I found a folding chair on the other side of the room to call home and get a good look at the room. A bookshelf spanned one of the walls from floor to ceiling, books crammed anywhere they'd fit. I'd neglected to take it all in during my tour a while back, but this time I took note of the colorful blue spines standing out among the other aged hardcover volumes. Interesting. They had light novels.

"Komari-san, are we allowed to—"

"*Bwuh?!* Huh?! What?!" She fumbled around for her phone. Now I just felt bad.

"Never mind. Read your book."

I scanned the shelves for an escape from the stifling awkwardness (and the boredom) and picked out something by Dazai. I was familiar in that I'd read some of his more famous works. He was a handsome guy, that Dazai. Surprisingly popular with the ladies. The image of a rushing river came to mind that I did not immediately cast away.

I flipped it open to a random page, shocked to find a modern-looking illustration. What scene was it from, I wondered. Some chapter called..."A Punishment Most Sweet." Whoever Takuya was, he apparently had a "raging sugarcane," and it was doing weird things to Haruta's "winking eye."

Wait a minute, this doesn't sound like Dazai.

Just as I was removing the dust jacket, the book flew from my hands. Komari held it tightly to her chest, staring at me like she'd seen a ghost.

"N-n-n-no boys allowed!" she sputtered.

"Why not? It's just Dazai Osamu."

"Not for boys!" Komari repeated. I wasn't even remotely following.

"I see the ice is broken," came a third voice.

A girl with long black hair in pigtails entered. She had a mature look about her that her glasses accentuated. Komari leaped behind her, leering back at me.

"Maybe not." Glasses Lady gently patted Komari on the head and smiled at me. "You must be Nukumizu-kun. Glad to see you again."

Her grin was contagious. I smiled back, relieved to meet someone sane for once.

"Oh, hi," I said. "Sorry I kind of ghosted you guys."

"I'm just happy you came back to us. Do you remember me? I'm the vice president, Tsukinoki Koto. A third-year."

"Yeah, I do, actually." I did not.

Tsukinoki-senpai looked over at the book in Komari's hands and nodded to herself. "Seems someone neglected to mention that all Dazai and Mishima works are off-limits to male club members," she explained.

"Mishima Yukio and Dazai Osamu? Both of them?" I asked.

The lenses of Tsukinoki-senpai's glasses flashed meaningfully. I did not know the significance of this, but my instincts were telling me to run.

Hands on each of my shoulders held me in place. "Wrong, my boy," Senpai said. "Dazai first. *Then* Mishima. Dazai Osamu ex Mishima Yukio. Not the other way around. There are no switches here, are we clear?" Her eyes implied there was only one answer to this question. I nodded out of fear for my life. "I'm glad we could reach an understanding. Now sit, and I'll get us some tea."

I'd spoken too soon. Sanity was clearly in short supply around here. I averted my gaze and stared idly at the zipper to my bag resting nearby, where no one could hurt me.

Komari tapped my shoulder to get my attention. She held out her phone. "I'm on your side. It's Mishima first. Mishima then Dazai."

This debate was not for me, unfortunately.

"What sorts of books catch your eye, Nukumizu-kun?" the vice president asked as she set the tea down.

"Uh, mostly light novels these days," I replied.

"Light novels, eh? Well, we've got plenty of those. Feel free to borrow any."

That was welcome news. Thanks to a certain someone, my shopping schedule had been thrown out of whack.

"So who are the other members?" I asked.

"The president's out right now, but there's him," Tsukinoki-senpai said. "He's the third-year who showed you around during the tour."

The description rang a bell. A tall, friendly, and handsome bell, as I recalled. Senpai took a sip of tea. Wait, was that it?

"Nothing like a hot cup of tea to spite the heat," she sighed.

"Are...are there any others?"

"Nope." She placed her cup on the table, grinning smugly for some reason. "The student council's been riding us about that lately. We'll need you to be present for the time being, at least until the heat dies down. You can help yourself to the tea, of course."

I glanced at the shelves full of light novels. I could live with that.

"If you say so," I sighed.

Tsukinoki-senpai grinned and then hopped up. "I should get going. Komari-chan, be a good host, will you?" Komari made a nasty grimace from behind her book. "That doofus Shintarou forgot he was on duty today, so I've gotta save his bacon."

She had a boyfriend, huh? These high schoolers and their hormones. It was like they always said: In junior high, romance was an elective. In high school, it was pretty much a prereq. Whoever "they" were. *Someone* had probably said it. Either way, I was missing that credit.

"And again." Tsukinoki-senpai stopped just before the door and turned around. "No Dazai or Mishima. I cannot stress that enough."

With a wave, she left. Not seconds later, there was another phone screen in my face that read, "Mishima THEN Dazai! Don't forget!"

Short on credits too, huh?

"I got it," I said. "Mind teaching me what this club's all about?"

"O-oh..." Komari made no effort to hide her displeasure.

"Who else am I gonna ask? The vice prez ran off to get her boyfriend or something."

"H-h-he isn't her boyfriend!" she yelped. "Sh-Shintarou is the club president. Tamaki Shintarou! They're just childhood friends!" She started fiercely typing something on her phone but froze midway. "M-my battery!"

Komari began rifling through the nearest bag, which happened to be mine. I was about to make a quip when a knock came at the door. When it rains, it pours.

"It's Shikiya," a voice said slowly. "Student council... Is now a good time?"

"Uh, not—"

I shut up as soon as she entered. She was like a flash-bang, her hair wavy, bright brown locks adorned with little flower accessories. Around one wrist she had a scrunchie, and both sets of nails were loudly decorated. Her unkempt uniform and short skirt hung loosely from her body. At a glance, you'd assume she'd gone light on the makeup, but her eyelashes definitely popped. The white colored contacts were a nightmarish touch to cap off the look.

This was a gyaru. A genuine, true, in-the-flesh fashion freak. And an existence far removed from my own.

Shikiya scanned the room, then marched up to me. I gulped. Whatever she wanted from me, it couldn't have been good. I was face-to-face with a *gyaru* of all things. My heart raced as I awaited the verbal lashing that was sure to come.

"Nukumizu-kun..." she breathed. "Club member?"

"Y-yes? That's me," I answered in the same sluggish way. This girl was throwing me off. This wasn't the energy I was expecting. Not that I was complaining.

"I apologize... My duties require me to be thorough," she said, slowly again. "Tell me... What sort of activities does the literature club conduct?" Shikiya-san leaned against a nearby wall like she was out of breath. I waffled between concern and confusion.

"I, uh, wouldn't really know."

"No? Are you...not a club member?" Her pale eyes pierced me.

Whoops. I'd nearly forgotten it was kind of my fault the lit club was under scrutiny to begin with. I looked to Komari for a lifeline. Unfortunately, she was too busy cowering in the corner, gripping her poor dead phone and shaking like a leaf. Very reassuring.

"Well, we're the lit club, so we, uh, read books," I said.

"*Just* read?" Shikiya-san tilted her head at me accusingly. What in the world else did these clubs do? "So...no activity."

She started to step closer, swaying, her steps deliberate yet unsteady. Why was today such a horror movie? Was zombie-aesthetic in or something?

"We write too!" I blurted. "Write stories and stuff!"

"You write?" she repeated. "So you don't just read." Shikiya-san looked up at the ceiling, pulled out a notebook, and jotted something down without even looking. "Noted... Thank you."

She shut the notebook with a thump before twirling around and leaving just as quickly as she'd arrived. It felt like I'd barely escaped with my life. Komari might not have been so lucky. She was absentmindedly tapping at the dead, black screen on her phone, and frankly, I didn't blame her. That crap had shaved days off my life span.

I knelt down to my bag, which had spilled onto the floor in the chaos, and grabbed my charger. I offered it to Komari.

"I-I need that!" She snatched it from me and, after a few failed attempts, plugged it into the wall with shaky hands.

And then it hit me. I was a pretty normal dude, thank you very much.

***

I scratched out an entry in my schedule. I was hunched over my desk that night, completely redoing all the plans I'd made. Some fiend named Yanami had thrown a wrench in my light novel purchasing agenda.

I leaned back, glanced at the collection in my room, and ran a few numbers in my head. Food expenses would be down, so I could funnel those funds into grabbing more new series if I slowed down on keeping up with ongoing stuff.

"I'll start with *Do You Love Your Big Sister and Her Close-Combat Skills?* for now. The anime was pretty good," I muttered.

Maybe this was a sign to get into *My Smol Senpai* finally. I'd been reserving shelf space for that plus the manga.

As I began to write, a small hand overlapped with mine. "*The Dark Maiden is an Innocent Mistress* must stay. Volume five is when my favorite character turns to evil."

"What are you doing in my room, Kaju?"

"I'm most places. You're just bad at noticing."

The freak was my little sister, Kaju. She was two years younger than me and actually pretty cute, just objectively. Not even from a brother's biased perspective. Last I'd heard, she had joined the student council too. The family resemblance was getting slimmer by the year.

"I've really got my eye on *My Smol Senpai*, though," I said.

"That one's good, but a little too naughty for my liking," said Kaju. "I don't approve of you consuming that sort of content, Oniisama."

"How do you even know that?"

"A friend let me borrow it. Too naughty."

What the heck, how come I didn't get to check it out? I silently complained.

Kaju stuffed my mouth full of cookies before I could vocalize my protests. Not bad. Next she forced my lips around a straw. Iced tea. I was feeling somewhat infantilized.

"I know how to drink things," I said.

Kaju stepped directly into my personal bubble. "Have you made any friends at school?"

"Uh, no?"

"I was afraid you'd say that," she sighed solemnly. "You worry me, Oniisama. You're in high school now. You're not allowed to have no friends anymore." I was officially an outlaw. "How many people did you even talk to today? Not counting teachers."

That was a good question. There was Yanami, Komari, Tsukinoki-senpai, Shikiya-san from the student council...

"About four," I replied.

"Four?" Kaju's eyes went wide as saucers. I was pretty proud of that number. She couldn't bring me down from this high. "Oniisama, having no friends is nothing to be ashamed of."

"You just said I'm not allowed."

"That doesn't hurt me. What hurts me is that you would *lie* to me. Your own flesh and blood."

"I...wasn't lying." She'd brought me down from that high.

"But what hurts me more is knowing *I* drove you to such tragic measures."

Kaju shoved yet more cookies into my mouth, tears pooling in her eyes.

"Kaju, please," I grunted through crumbs.

"It'll be okay, Oniisama." She held me oh so tenderly in her arms. In the height of summer. It was way too hot for this. "I'll find some friends for you. I promise."

Nukumizu Kaju—obsessive brother-lover or just a worry-wart? I wasn't sure how to frame it. Either way, this was par for the course for her.

Was having no friends really so terrible? I wasn't unhappy or anything, personally. Aside from little things, like not hearing about schedule changes (which would occasionally make me late to class) and being unintentionally excluded from most communication, I didn't much care.

I sipped some more iced tea, grateful, at least, that things couldn't possibly get any worse.

Current tab: 3,617 yen.

***

The next day, lunchtime. I had come to the fire escape to get my bento, only to be immediately accosted.

"Gee, *thanks.*"

"Who? Me?"

"Yes, *you.*" I had hardly spoken a word and Yanami was already most displeased. "Remember when I asked for your help yesterday? Karaoke? No? Well, guess what. It sucked."

Yanami sat next to me, only adding to my confusion. I didn't realize this was going to be a whole thing.

"What do you want me to do about that?"

"Sometimes all a girl wants is a little validation," Yanami grumbled. "That *Frozen* duet straight up traumatized me."

I searched my memory. "Oh, did they do that one that goes 'let it snow' or whatever?"

She gave me a look. Not quite, it seemed. "No, they did the song that Anna and the prince sing together. That bit at the end, oh my *god*. I didn't think I'd make it."

"The part where he goes, 'Can I say something crazy? Will you marry me?'" That one I remembered.

"And then Anna's all like, 'Can I say something even crazier? Yes!'" Yanami reenacted with a wispy cadence. She threw her head in her hands and wailed a wail that would have put the damned to shame. She was just torturing herself at this point. "She's doing it on purpose, I tell you. She's trying to break me, that...that ice queen."

"Y-you know how couples are. It's just the honeymoon phase," I said. "Anyway, did you bring lunch?"

Cards on the table, I was pretty excited and couldn't wait much longer. Could anyone blame me? A homemade bento from a classmate, a girl no less, was plenty justification for a little impatience.

"Here," she mumbled.

The bento box—if it could even be called that—was a colorful mosaic of what looked to be paper. On top, I could make out text reading, "Thighs—98 Yen." The thing was made of carefully folded fliers. Reminded me of some craft project I'd see at my grandma's.

"What am I looking at?" I asked.

"The plan was to just make your portion while I cooked mine this morning. I did mean to, really."

"Okay. And?"

"My mom saw me going for a second bento box and said Sousuke was a 'lucky guy'..."

Oof, that was a gut punch. Moms really knew how to make it sting.

I maintained a respectful silence as I opened up the "bento." Inside was but a lone sandwich wrapped in plastic. "This is from the convenience store."

"Uh, yeah, were you even listening? I couldn't make you anything with my mom breathing down my neck!"

The only thing homemade about this lunch was the packaging it came in.

"Sooo, how much do you think for this?" Yanami asked.

"Let's say...268 yen," I said.

"Yikes, okay."

Hey, I was just reading the label. She scooped up a piece of fried egg from her own lunch and plopped it into my box.

"We'll call that 300." I pulled away when she tried to test her luck with karaage next. That girl wasn't gonna upcharge me. "Back to the first topic, it sounds like those two really just need some space. You've got plenty of other friends to hang out with, don't you?"

I tossed the fried egg into my mouth. A little burnt but not bad. The Yanamis liked their eggs on the sweet side.

"They can get...weird." She started languidly mangling the rest of her eggs. Another victim. "It was always just Sousuke and me before Karen-chan transferred in. When I'm not with him, it's like, people start making assumptions."

"Oh," I said. "I'm, uh, not sure what to say."

Plop. Karaage into my box.

"How much?"

I stared at the fried chicken, and it stared back, mocking me for my naivety. "350."

"Where'd you go after school yesterday, anyway?" Yanami asked. "I saw you leave a different way from usual."

"You keep tabs on me?"

"I mean, bit hard not to notice the guy beelining for the door by himself every day."

There was never any bite to her words, and yet they consistently wounded me. No more, though. I chewed smugly on a mouthful of sandwich, safe in the knowledge that such conspicuous days were behind me.

"Turns out I'm in the literature club," I said. "I'll be hanging around there for a while, I guess."

"Huh. Didn't know you were into that sorta thing." Yanami munched on an octopus-shaped sausage. "Maybe I'll come check it out too. You mind?"

"Not really. Didn't know *you* were into that sorta thing."

"I like flowers just fine, thank you."

"Literature. Not horticulture," I enunciated.

Maybe I did understand how she got rejected after all. A grain of rice clung to her cheek.

***

The bell chimed. School was out. One's first instinct would naturally be to book it, but hark, this was folly. The secret to the art of departure was patience. Danger lurked in a school of freshly liberated students, particularly at the doors. Social groups often picked these areas to loiter so as to ensure a pack didn't leave without all of its respective members. They would not budge for a lowly background extra such as myself. 'Twas a vicious cycle, the life of one of the B-cast. One without escape.

I lazily gathered my things, keeping a close eye on the flow of people. The door was largely clear, but this was a trap. The pack remained. They had simply relocated to the shoe cupboards at the school entrance, where the loneliest and most stubborn of the bunch would often congregate. Worst-case scenario, they were gathered in front of my cupboard, and biding my time by pretending to forget which was mine wouldn't fly this late into the semester.

Actually, come to think of it, I wasn't supposed to leave today. It had completely slipped my mind that I was in the literature club now. For the time being, at least.

A man suddenly slipped into the classroom and came straight up to my desk. "Hey, Nukumizu-kun. I hear you're in the lit club?"

"Huh?"

Ayano Mitsuki was his name, another familiar face from the same junior high as me. I wouldn't have called us "friends," per se. We'd just gone to the same cram school together, so we were technically on speaking terms. For the record, his grades were better than mine, and yes, he had glasses.

"Yeah?" I said. "I guess I am."

"One of my teachers told me you guys have an Abe Kobo collection there," said Ayano. "Could I swing by to borrow it sometime?"

I wouldn't have known. All I'd cared to note were the light novels.

"Uhhh, probably. I'd have to ask my senpai."

"I appreciate it." He flashed a grin you just couldn't hate, dropped a hand on my shoulder, and then made to saunter back toward the door.

Just then, a blur of golden brown spawned out of thin air in the corner of my periphery.

Yakishio Lemon thumped her tanned arms down onto my desk. "Hold up, Mitsuki!" She leaned in uncomfortably close, a mixture of 8×4 brand deodorant and sweat dominating my senses. Why me? "The team's off today, so I was wondering if maybe you wanted to grab something to eat or whatever?"

"Sorry." Ayano held his hands together in apology. "I've got cram school today."

"Aww, c'mon!" Yakishio moaned. "We're first-years. Don't you know that all study and no play makes Jack a dumb boy?"

"I'd do a little less play and a little more studying unless you plan on being a first-year forever."

Now they were just flirting. Right in front of me. Awesome.

Another girl poked her head into the class. "Mitsuki-san, we're going to be late."

I recognized her. She and Ayano had spent a lot of time together back when we shared a cram school. Her looks and grades had made her a bit of a celebrity at the time. Never would have guessed we went to the same high school.

"I'll be right there, Chihaya," Ayano said. "Later, Lemon."

"Oh..." A rain cloud rolled in over Yakishio. "Okay. Bye." She waved at him, slowly and lifelessly.

I was at my limit and ready to dip, but Yakishio was making that difficult given she was blocking me from grabbing my bag.

"E-excuse me. Yakishio-san?" I said. "I, uh, need my..."

"Hey, Nukumizu, are you and Mitsuki friends? I don't *think* you were in our class last year." She blinked at me, her long eyelashes far too close for comfort.

Yakishio Lemon was the star of the track team, their best sprinter, and arguably the star of the classroom as well. People gravitated to her. She had short hair, a gentle face, and the kind of toned figure and sun-kissed skin that could have stolen anyone's breath away.

Once I'd recomposed myself, I said, "I, er, wouldn't call us *friends*. We just went to the same cram school. Sometimes we talk."

Yakishio's eyes lit up. "Ohhh, I getcha! So you know who that girl is?!" She shoved her face right up to mine, throwing my poise to the wind yet again.

"A-Asagumo-san, I think her name is. They were in the accelerated course together. Pretty equal on grades, from what I remember."

"O-oh. Okay." She stared vacantly in the direction Ayano had left in. "I wonder if he likes smart girls better..."

Am I crazy, or...?

"To clarify," I said, "they were together a lot, but they just looked like friends to me. Same course is all."

"You're so right!" Yakishio cheered. "I so got friend vibes too!"

She beamed like the sun. I chose not to touch on the question of their relationship *outside* of what I'd seen.

"Can I get my bag?" I asked.

"Oh, sorry. You know what? A good old-fashioned sprint should clear my head!"

She wasted no time and started stretching on the spot, her bronze limbs bare for all to see, before bolting out the door. I at last reached down for my bag and stood.

So many people, so many stories happening all around me, and I'd been none the wiser. My one wish was that I could at least continue to avoid the drama and live out my days in relative peace.

"Done with your chat, playboy?" With perfect contradictory timing, Yanami appeared behind me.

"Can I help you?" I said.

None of this made sense. First Yakishio, then Yanami. All the prettiest girls in school were practically lining up just to bug me. I braced my wallet for yet another loan.

Yanami smiled at me innocently. "We're going to that club, aren't we? I did say I was coming."

I hadn't believed her. Yanami Anna and books went together about as well as water and oil, I imagined. Still, it wasn't my place to tell her no.

I nodded.

***

"You're sure you're sure?" I asked on our way to the club room. "It's not exactly a party where we're going. It might not be your thing."

A day was all it took to learn what I needed about the lit club. And what I learned was that it wasn't exactly where the cool kids hung out.

"Eh, I'm sure it'll be fine. I used to do needle felting," Yanami insisted. "That thing where you poke wool a whole bunch to make cute little dudes."

"Again, literature. We are going to the *literature* club. Not the little-dudes club."

Forget it. She wasn't worth the energy. I opened the door.

I paused. "Oh, hello."

"Nukumizu-kun." Tsukinoki-senpai brushed a lock of hair behind her ear without looking up from her book. "Good to see you."

Komari glanced, frowned at me, and then froze upon noticing the stranger with me.

"She's with me. Wanted to have a look at the club," I explained.

"Hiya. Hope I'm not a bother," she said. "I'm Yanami. Nukumizu-kun and I are in the same class."

"Welcome, welcome! I'll get us some tea." The vice president jumped up, adjusting her glasses, and nudged me as she passed me by. "Nice catch. She's a cutie."

"R-right..." I said.

"She your girlfriend?" Tsukinoki-senpai asked out loud.

Oh, Jesus Christ.

"N-no, we're—"

"Oh, no, no," Yanami butted in. "Just classmates." There was nothing on her face. No hint of emotion. No hesitation, not even displeasure. She may as well have been commenting on the weather. The moment came and went like dust on the wind. She was then quickly preoccupied with surveying the room. "You guys sure keep a lotta books around here. What for?"

Suddenly, it was like you could hear a pin drop. Senpai and Komari stared holes through me, their expressions completely deadpan.

Just as the atmosphere was becoming crushing, the door swung open. "Whoa, we havin' a party?"

A fairly tall man entered. The president, if I had to guess. Tamaki Shintarou—my savior.

"Well, well. Look who decided to show up." Tsukinoki-senpai made her best attempt at a wrinkly scowl, only to be betrayed by her own upturned lips.

"Cut me some slack." The president put a suave hand on her shoulder. "I've been studying for exams."

"Uh-huh. And I'm the queen of France."

"What, you don't believe me? Oh, hey, Nukumizu-kun. Good to see you again. And who's that? A new member?"

"Just here to check things out," said Yanami. "Nice to meet you. I'm Yanami."

Tamaki-senpai welcomed her with a smile, stepping toward us. "Make yourself at home."

Before he could make it far, Komari jumped out in front of him. "P-P-Prez, I—" she stammered. "I r-read the book you lent me! It was good!"

"Already? Dang, glad you liked it," Tamaki-senpai said. "Koto over here just doesn't respect sci-fi." He gestured to her with his thumb.

The vice president shot him back a look. "I respect the genre well enough. It's *you* who won't read Haruki."

"Since when were you a Harukist?"

"I'm not *that* into him. You're still sitting on that Usami Rin novel I gave you, by the way."

"Hey, I finished that! Boy, did that idol burn."

They were so a thing that it wasn't even funny. I let my eyelids hang, unamused, while they went off.

"I-I, um... I like Egan!" Komari interjected. What a trooper. "Even if he's a bit...c-confusing."

"For real?" said Tamaki-senpai. "I knew one of us had good taste!"

The president ruffled her hair. She yiped.

Tsukinoki-senpai swatted his hand away. "Are you *trying* to get #MeToo'd? You just let me know if he's getting too handsy, Komari-chan. I'll set him straight."

"I-I don't...!" Komari jumped at the volume of her own voice and hung her head. "I...don't mind." Her cheeks turned bright red.

"Look at her, Koto. Why can't you be that adorable?" Tamaki-senpai teased.

Groaning, Tsukinoki-senpai said, "You really shouldn't spoil him. He'll let anything go to his head if you're not careful."

The president glanced at his watch and sucked air through his teeth. "I gotta get going. There's a meeting for club presidents, and I'm cutting it close. At least I get to brag about our new visitor."

"I'll come with," said Tsukinoki-senpai. "You'll curl up somewhere and fall asleep on the way there otherwise."

"You're my favorite alarm clock, Koto."

"We'll see how you feel after I sign you up for janitor duty."

The two left, their casual flirting echoing down the hallway and through the door. Leaving the rest of us to wonder what the point of that entire display had even been.

"H-he called me… The president…called me cute." Komari was mumbling and giggling to herself, off in her own little world. Poor thing had no idea.

Yanami tapped me on the shoulder and furtively leaned in close. Very close. Oh god, I could smell her. "So, the prez and vice prez. They're totally dating, right?"

"Dunno. Wouldn't be surprised," I replied.

Komari, with her sonar hearing, thrust her phone out at us. The screen read, "They are NOT dating! They are childhood FRIENDS!"

"Childhood friends?" Yanami narrowed her eyes like an activated sleeper agent.

"Yes! JUST friends!" Komari's phone screen asserted.

Her nose scrunched, nostrils flared, and piece—well, not *said*, technically—either way, Komari stormed back to her book and shoved a pair of blaring earbuds into her ears. There was grumpy, and then there was her.

Yanami noisily scooched a nearby chair over to sit in. "What's the phone about? She just do that?" she asked. I had no answer. "Anyway. So childhood friends, huh?"

"What? Oh. Right. Guess they are," I said.

"Wonder what makes *her* so special," Yanami muttered grimly.

"Innocent until proven guilty, Yanami-san."

"Wait a second..." She slowly, dramatically raised her head. Her eyes landed on Komari. "Homewrecker," she growled. Komari twitched.

"Okay, relax, we just established they aren't dating. How does that make her a homewrecker?"

"It's not about dating or not dating. As far as I'm concerned, any floozy that steps in on a man with a childhood friend is a dirty thief. How is that not obvious?"

I pictured a yuri couple. Many would rage and froth at the mouth at the mere suggestion of including a man in such a relationship. That made it click for me. Death was too light a punishment.

"Okay, I get it," I confessed, "but let's put a pin in that. Komari-san's literally right there."

"She's got music on. She can't hear."

We turned to her. Komari seemed to shrink away, like she could feel us staring. Something didn't feel right.

"What if she isn't?" I said.

"But she's got earbuds in," said Yanami.

"She could be pretending to listen to music so she can eavesdrop on us."

"Didn't you hear it earlier, though?"

"Yeah, but do you hear it *now*? We've been hoodwinked, Yanami-san."

The sweat of a liar poured from Komari's face. She took out her earbuds, holding me in her disgruntled gaze, and handed me something. "S-spare key. Forgot."

"Oh. Thanks."

"I-I'mma g-go home now!" And out she flew, tripping over her own legs.

The quiet was sudden and overwhelming. Only two remained: the outsider and the technically-not-really outsider. What was there to even do? I couldn't give much of an overview of the club, because I hadn't been given one myself.

"Guess I'll make some tea," I said. "Write your name on the visitors list."

"Thanks. Get me green," Yanami replied. She signed her name and started flipping pages. "Lotsa people on here. Oh, there's you. And there's that one girl. Komari-san."

Yanami quickly grew bored with the list and browsed the shelves. I prayed she'd stay away from anything Dazai or Mishima. For both our sakes.

"Tea," I said, placing her cup down.

"Thanks. By the way..." She took a sip and stared me dead in the eye. "What club is this again?"

***

"I'm like some *normal teenager*," I mumbled to myself.

The most use I had ever gotten out of LINE was stamp packs of my favorite characters (for the novelty). Now, I lay there, sprawled out on the living room sofa, an actual message in my notifications. A spirited welcome from Tsukinoki-senpai.

I had joined the lit club group chat. My high school career had truly peaked, but I honestly didn't mind getting off the ride here.

A humble life was all I craved. A chill one. Like that of a clam. Those guys were chill.

I remembered Ayano asking about borrowing some books. A good enough excuse for my first message.

"A guy I know wants to borrow the Abe Kobo collection. That cool?" I echoed out loud as I typed. Weirdly enough, I sorta understood why old folk did that so much.

Here began the true test. Would I actually get a reply? I'd heard of getting "left on read" before. What if everyone had straight up blocked me?

The notif came. Phew. Not blocked.

‹Tsukino-Mono: Absolutely. An addendum, however: Let not this fish escape our net.›

The rest of whatever that was aside, I'd gotten my permission. I resumed my lazy idling. Not long after, Kaju strolled over and sat down across the coffee table.

"You are a beautiful person, Oniisama."

"Thanks?"

"You're such a good listener, and you always make me feel like I have worthwhile things to say."

"Except for the times I call you out." Like just then, as a matter of fact.

"You're so patient," Kaju went on. "You're never short with me or my antics."

"So you're aware that they are, in fact, antics."

She cleared her throat all formal-like. "Anyway, we're going to make a charaben."

I was speechless. For once, I had no quips. She had won.

"Right," I finally said. "You lost me. Little more context please."

"You're scaring me, Oniisama. You've been lying there smiling at your anime characters all day."

There was the "character" part of charaben.

"Still lost."

"We should funnel those emotions into something productive," Kaju said. "We'll make a bento in the style of some popular anime or manga, and then people will talk to you!"

"Why specifically anime or manga?"

"Because that's the only thing you can hold a conversation about?"

She wasn't wrong. She really wasn't. Still rude.

"Who am I eating with that's gonna look over and be like, 'Wow, look at this guy, he's got a charaben'?"

"Please, Oniisama. I know you're friendless, but surely even *you* eat lunch with people."

"Nope, not really."

"You… What?" Kaju put her hand to her mouth. Disbelief filled her eyes. "But don't you ask anyone? All you have to do is ask, you know?" Therein lay the crux of the issue, my dear sister. "Do you need me at school with you? I'll go. I'll ask for you."

"Whatever social life I even remotely had before would be smithereens if you did that," I said.

"Charaben it is. Here, I made a test sample." She produced a bento box and lifted the lid. "I thought your face would be a good place to start. Help smooth along introductions." It was a work of art. Like, genuinely, this went beyond a cute food gimmick. The realism was a little unnerving. "I used sesame to write an informative profile about you. You'll be the king of school in no time."

Somehow, I doubted my classmates would be very interested in my height, weight, and first crush.

"Why did you put *you* for my first crush?" I asked.

"I don't understand. You've been calling me cute since before I can remember, Oniisama."

As brothers often did for their sisters.

"I won't be needing a bento for a while anyway," I said. "Someone's already making lunch for me."

"Someone—" Kaju froze and started bugging out. "What? Who? What?"

"Uh, hello? You in there?"

"Oniisama!" Kaju shrieked. "Do you mean to tell me that, before any friends at all, you've made a *girl*friend?! Without my permission?!"

"Relax, she's not my girlfriend! We'd have to be *friends* first, and we both know I don't have any of those!"

"Right, of course. How silly of me. That would just be ridiculous." She didn't have to twist the knife. "I've heard stories of people starting relationships with individuals of questionable tangibility. Particularly people with your interests. Though I have to express my concern for your nutritional intake if these 'bento' are of similar physicality."

"You really have no faith in me, do you?" I said. "It's a real person making real food, for your information."

In fact, you could even sell it in convenience stores.

"My question is still how a friendless, girlfriendless boy such as yourself just happens upon a supply of bento."

"It's been paid for," I said.

"Ah." Kaju clapped her hands together like she'd solved the case of the century. "I've heard from friends that some women *have* been adding bento boxes to their services lately."

"You have questionable friends."

I stared down at my seaweed self. He stared back. We shared a common understanding.

Current tab: 3,267 yen.

***

The following afternoon, Wednesday, Yanami met me at the fire escape again right on time. This "bartering" thing was happening after all.

My not-friend-not-girlfriend spread her handkerchief over one of the steps before taking a seat and sighing. "It's happening again. This time Karen-chan wants me to join them at her place for a study sesh."

"You can always tell her no," I said.

In response to the objectively best advice she could have possibly received, Yanami scowled in disgust. "And leave those two alone together?!" she shouted.

"They're already dating. We're past the point of that being concerning."

This could never be simple, could it? I couldn't just take my lunch and be done with it. There was always something.

"She wants me gone for good. I'm telling you," Yanami started raving. "She knows this thirst can't be quenched with water."

Some thoughts are best kept to ourselves, I thought decidedly to myself.

"You can't keep assuming the worst," I said. "She probably just thinks it'd be too awkward to be alone together, so she wants you there to lighten the mood."

"So I'm the bait, and Sousuke's the prey."

I'd stepped on a land mine. "No, that's not what I'm—"

"I make it seem simple. I lower his guard, and once she's got him in her room..." Yanami batted her eyelashes at me. "'Oh, gee whiz, it seems like Anna-chan won't make it,'" she cooed, her voice pitched up.

"Excuse me?"

"We're acting. Play along. It's Karen-chan and Sousuke alone in her room."

"Okay?"

I wasn't sure why she needed *me* to reenact her worst nightmares.

"From the top. 'Oh, gee whiz, it seems like Anna-chan won't make it,'" she cooed. "Now you, Nukumizu-kun. You're Sousuke. Go!"

"Uh... 'Really? I guess that means it's just us,'" I said in a voice.

This is so dumb.

"'What if I said'"—Yanami cast her eyes down and cuddled up against me—"'I kept her away on purpose?'"

I dug through the annals of my mind. I'd seen and read enough rom-coms to know what came next.

"'What if I said I had a feeling and came anyway?'"

"'Sousuke...'"

"'Karen...'"

We gazed at each other for a beat, and a beat later Yanami zipped back upright and smacked her knees. "I *knew* it! She's after his chastity, that witch!"

In your dreams, I have no doubt.

"Anyway, my lunch?" I said.

"You realize this is why you have no friends, right?" With that helpful little gem, Yanami pulled out an aluminum bento box—just the one. "Hold the lid," she said.

I did. Yanami stabbed her chopsticks into the rice.

"What are you doing?" I asked.

"Remember what I said yesterday? Can't bring two boxes." She shakily hoisted up a chunk of rice, then dunked it into the lid I was holding. The glob had quite a bit of weight to it. It looked halfway to mochi. "My plan this time was to just try and cram lunch for two into this one. More coming."

The next two servings, meat and veggies both, were hard, firm blocks, molded into the shape of the bento box. "Appetizing" didn't describe it well.

"You can eat now," said Yanami.

"Oh, uh, thanks."

I contemplated how exactly to tackle the rice glob for a moment. Chopsticks failed. The juices from the meat looked promising, though, so I softened and mixed the ball up in that. Progress was being made at last.

"Good?" she asked. Ballsy move, given the state everything was in.

"You made all of this?"

"Yup. And I didn't skimp or nothin'," she claimed proudly. "So how much?"

Thank god this wasn't just like Mama used to make, or I'd have had questions about her childhood. I noted a bit of premade croquette in one of the cubes.

"Hm. 400 yen," I said.

"Nice. I'll take it." Yanami chomped into her rice glob, blissfully unaware that I was being nice with that appraisal. Granted, there was a lot of it. "Might even have it all paid back before summer vacation."

She was right. Couldn't forget that these little get-togethers were temporary—only until she'd covered what she owed me. Which was whatever. The time limit made it bearable, maybe even enjoyable in the moment. Not that I'd let her off the hook early.

Yanami lidded her now-empty bento box sometime later and stood up. "Wanna head upstairs? There's a really nice view of campus from there."

I couldn't think of a reason to refuse, so I followed. From up top, beneath a cloudless July sky, we could make out the track team mid-practice.

"Hey, that looks like Lemon-chan." Yanami leaned against the rail and pointed. There was no mistaking that tanned figure. She broke away almost immediately, leaving her peers in the dust. "Man, she's fast."

The type of person who could spend their fifty-minute break eating, changing, practicing, and then changing again could *not* be me. And not in a derogatory way. Watching them just felt like watching birds fly.

"She won the hundred meter in that city-wide rookie race," I said. "Even placed in the inter-high prelims."

"You know a lot about her." The noticeboard did, at least. And I knew a lot about that. "Lemon-chan's so incredible."

It was mindless banter. So I started to make a mindless reply. When I saw her, though, I swallowed it back down.

Tears swelled in the corners of her eyes. One fell and trickled down her cheek, glistening in the sun, before the wind carried it away. There was nothing manufactured about this expression. No goofy non sequiturs were on her lips. A girl I barely knew was crying in front of me, and I didn't know what to do. Time felt like jelly. Thick and slow yet impossible to grasp.

"Y-Yanami-san, are you okay?" I managed to ask.

"He didn't pick me," she croaked. A late realization. "Yeah, yeah. Bit late, I know."

"H-how'd you know I was thinking that?"

Private minds were not for public reading.

"Because I'm thinking it too," she said. "It's setting in."

"I...don't follow."

"Just, watching Lemon-chan run. Moving forward," she went on. "And I'm not." More tears shimmered when she blinked. "I missed my chance. I knew that day one. I think I just needed time for it to...feel real, you know?"

Yakishio darted off the starting line again, this time against the boys. One of the tall ones outpaced her right at the last minute.

"It's hard to put into words. I think you'd understand if you ever had your heart broken one day," Yanami said.

"You think?" I replied.

"Rejection is rejection. Hurts for everyone, and you'll never get any closure." She stretched out wide. "But the world keeps turning. People keep running. So all you can do is try to keep up."

So sorta like a special scene auto-triggering in a game, I rationalized.

"Yeah, I wouldn't know. Never been rejected," I said with a dash of self-deprecation.

Yanami smirked at me. "Nice humblebrag, bro."

A light novel protagonist would have known the right words to say in that moment to sweep the heroine off her feet. I didn't, and this wasn't a heroine. It was a loser. A loser who had to go on living while the clock kept ticking, and the one who got away kept making memories with a girl who wasn't her.

We watched them run. The breeze filled the silence.

Current tab: 2,867 yen.

Too Many Losing Heroines!

INTERMISSION

Even Though She Was Hungry—She Was a Good Girl, an Angel

A MECHANICAL *BEEP* SOUNDED FROM THE RICE cooker on a dimly lit countertop. A pajama-clad Yanami Anna made no effort to stifle her yawn as she peeked into the fridge.

"Eggs and not much else."

In the crisper drawer she found some shriveling komatsuna spinach and half a pack of ham. Only frozen pasta and some ice cream greeted her in the freezer. Some extra excavating, however, managed to unearth an opened bag of mixed vegetables.

"Maybe I can work with this?"

Yanami Anna laid out her spoils: eggs, ham, mixed veggies, and some yellowing spinach. She gnawed on her ice cream bar pensively. Cooking was by no means her strong suit, but a certain fussy boy's lack of enthusiasm had gotten under her skin.

"Since he wants to play that game..."

An idea. Yanami swung open a cupboard. Past an assortment of canned goods originating from all manner of places and times, she pulled out a particularly dusty one from the back. Its label read thusly: "Imperial Hotel—Special White Sauce."

This would do nicely. It was grand—it was *special*—it would break that jerk's poker face for sure. Yanami eyed her secret ingredient with pride, until she noticed the best-by date hidden at the edge of the label.

What year is it again? she wondered. *Reiwa started in 2019, so...*

That was close enough for Yanami. She clunked the can down onto the table. If a guy like Napoleon could make or eat canned food—she couldn't remember which—a hundred years ago, what was one or two past the date in modern times?

Yanami took a chunk out of her ice cream, satisfied with her theory. Then she knelt down on the dark kitchen floor, held her head, and made a closed-mouth shriek into the lonely silence.

And so that summer night went on for fifteen-year-old Yanami Anna and her hypersensitive teeth.

LOSS 2

Yakishio Lemon versus the Narrative

SO MANY CICADAS. THE CRIES WERE DEAFENING. And the sweltering sun didn't help matters. Second period—PE—was finally over, and all that stood in the way between me and freedom was cleanup duty.

I dropped the last hurdle into the storage shed and wiped up some of the sweat dripping from my face. The system was broken. It just wasn't fair that the guy on duty had to be whoever's seating number *happened* to match up with the day of the month. Whoever decided that little rule must have been number thirty and thought himself real clever.

"I'll kill 'em," I grumbled, beating the dirt off my hands.

The sooner I wrapped this up, the sooner I could get out of these gross, sweaty clothes. The last guy to change was the last one to stand around in his underwear while everyone else was dressed, and I wasn't looking to be that guy.

Suddenly, the door rattled shut. The place went dark. Had it finally happened? Was the bullying finally starting? This was it for me.

I whipped around to find that I wasn't alone. Standing there in the dim darkness, fidgeting awkwardly, was Yakishio Lemon. Sweat gripped her clothes, gluing them to her body and accentuating her figure.

"Yakishio-san?" I said.

This was a scene straight out of an anime. I gulped.

Yakishio avoided looking me in the eye. She brushed back a strand of hair clinging to her cheek and stepped closer. "Hey, Nukumizu," she said. "I wanted to ask you something."

"Oh. Okay."

Unlike those with minds of a lesser discipline, my expectations weren't high. I'd seen enough rom-coms to know that we hadn't had nearly enough buildup to unlock a scene of this caliber.

"Have you guys talked since?" she asked.

"Huh? Who? About what?"

This was no romantic development. This was the kind where the lead is expected to act all flustered before his hopes are dashed. I could handle that.

"Mitsuki," Yakishio said. "About the books. Did he come get 'em yet?"

Come to think of it, I hadn't updated Ayano at all about that.

Yakishio held her hands behind her back and shyly tapped at the ground with the tip of her shoe. "I-I was thinking that, well, maybe I could make the delivery myself?"

"I mean, it's a pretty big collection," I said. "It'd make more sense to have him come and..." Yakishio kept fidgeting. I caught on. "Actually, let him know for me, would you? I got permission, so he can stop by whenever."

"Can do! You've got my word he'll get the word!" Her smile lit up the shed. The dust dancing in the beams of sunlight seemed to almost sparkle around her. "I'll let him know to come by after school!"

"Actually, wait. I have an idea."

"Yeah?" Yakishio tilted her head, still smiling.

We came from the same junior high. The sentimental side of me felt like doing her a favor.

"How about you tell him to come by on a day you don't have practice?" I said.

It was the perfect setup to get them together for longer. Maybe I could even work something out and get them the room to themselves for a couple hours.

"But why, though?" Yakishio said, peering confusedly at me.

"So you can, er, come take a tour of the club. On the same day," I said. I couldn't possibly have made it clearer. "You know."

"Not...really."

Screw it.

"You *could* just tell him to come pick up his books and be done with it," I explained. "Or you could pick a day you don't have practice so you can come together. If you don't know how to invite yourself along, the tour gives you an excuse to be there anyway."

She clapped her hands together and raised her eyebrows in realization. "Oh, I get it! You're a smart guy, Nukumizu." Her lips spread into a wide grin. She smacked me on the back. "I had you all wrong. You're not so bad!"

I wasn't sure I wanted to know what all these "ideas" my classmates kept alluding to were.

"D-don't get it twisted, though!" Yakishio said hastily. "Mitsuki's just a friend, y'know? We're just bros, that's all!"

"Nice save," I said with a dry expression.

Yakishio pouted at me. Ranking in the social hierarchy didn't equate to emotional maturity, it seemed.

"Anyway, can we, like, wrap this up? I'm melting over here." She fanned her shirt at the collar. Meanwhile, I forced myself to bite my tongue. She tried the door. "Uh..."

"What?" I tried the door with her. No dice.

Yakishio turned to me. "I, uh, think we might, maybe, possibly be locked inside."

"You're joking," I said. "Help! Is anyone out—"

"Shush!" Yakishio hissed. "Stop yelling!"

She swung one arm around my neck from behind and held on for dear life. The many things pressing against my back almost made me forget about all the nasty sweat she was covered in. Almost.

"Can't...breathe!" I choked. Try as I might to throw her off, it was her muscles against my lack-thereof. "I see a light...!"

I tapped her arm.

"Oh, shoot, sorry," she said. "You okay?"

"You... You're insane," I panted. "Why the actual hell did you stop me?"

"Because Mitsuki's class had PE too! He could be out there!"

"And we didn't call for him because...?"

"Because!" Yakishio asserted. "Wh-what if he saw me alone in here with another guy and he, well, I dunno..." She twiddled her thumbs. I would have found it cute in any other situation.

"Well, we've gotta hurry before everyone leaves," I said.

"The next class'll show up soon enough, okay? Let's just wait till then."

"And then they'll find a guy and a girl who've been alone together for God knows how long."

"You could cross-dress," Yakishio proposed.

"If that's on the table, you'd sell it better anyway."

We were getting nowhere, and all our classmates had left in the meantime. The murmurs of students had been replaced by a cacophony of cicadas.

Yakishio hoisted herself up to peek out a high window. "Huh. Why's no one coming?"

"Oh," I said. "Yakishio-san. I think they might be at the pool."

"Huh?" The bell sounded. The next period had started. "Why weren't *we* at the pool?!"

"Didn't you hear the teacher? The second-years were using it to practice for the meet."

"Oh. Right. So *now* the pool's open," Yakishio said. "And we're stuck out here."

The cicadas buzzed their orchestra.

"Help!" Yakishio cried. "I'm in here too!"

"Someone!" I shouted.

Our pleas echoed out into nothingness. Eventually, we gave up and found a couple comfortable spots on the ground to contemplate.

The forecast this morning had said today would be a scorcher—a high of thirty-five degrees—and the shed was only getting hotter. I stopped feeling quite as sweaty at some point, not because I'd gotten used to the heat, but because I was as dry as a skeleton.

"Wonder when someone'll notice," I mumbled.

"The track team'll be here at lunch at least," Yakishio panted. An actual, visible puddle was forming around her. Her body was a machine.

"Hey, are you okay?"

"Yeah, nah, I'm an impala kind of girl. No gazelle here," she muttered.

"Oh, cool."

Wait, what?

"I try to tell people, four legs are better than one. But do they listen?" she rambled. "Listen. Nothing cools ya down like water does a spotted hyena."

"Yakishio-san?"

She was anything but okay. I had to do something.

The window was high up, close to the ceiling, and barred for safety. Couldn't squeeze through there. I dug around the shelves to maybe find something to make noise with—a whistle or megaphone maybe—and found an old, dusty duffel bag buried deep. Inside were women's clothes, a towel, and, thank god, a half-drunk bottle of water.

My stomach dropped. The liquid was coated with sheets of mold. I shoved the bottle back in the bag, then happened to spot a can of cooling spray.

"Yakishio-san! This should help," I said.

She noticed the can, and a little light returned to her eyes. "You're the best, Nukkun! Hit me."

Nukkun?

She turned her back to me, throwing off her drenched top. The sports bra concealed very little of her bare skin, even in the dim light.

I choked on spit. "S-slow down!"

"But I *neeed* it!" Yakishio whined.

To think I would live to see the day a woman begged me for something—and for this, no less. Timidly, I gave her back a good spritz. Yakishio let out several less than wholesome moans and yips in the process.

"Front next," she said.

She turned. Was this allowed? It felt like I was breaking something. A law, a rule of some kind. I could see her naked stomach, and the tan lines peeking out from her sports bra weren't helping with the intrusive thoughts.

I sprayed. Her abs twitched. She moaned again. It was not my fault for the places my mind went. That was a hill I would die on.

"Better?" I asked.

"A little," she said. She still looked vacant, her eyes unsteady. Her hands went under her bra.

"Wait, wait, wait!" I blurted. "Keep that on!"

"Aww, c'mon, Nukkun. We're both girls here. I'm sooo sweaty. Gimme a towel."

This girl had gone delusional. She thought she was in the girls' locker room, of all places.

I ruffled through the bag for the towel and, keeping my eyes firmly pointed in the other direction, handed it to Yakishio as she tossed her bra to the side. "P-put that back on when you're done!"

"Hey," she said, "that's my bag. So this is where I lost it."

Yakishio took a gander inside while she wiped herself down.

"Yakishio-san!" I shouted. "C-clothes! Clothes first!"

"I left a drink inside too!"

Uh-oh. I risked a peek to find Yakishio moments before taking a sip out of the moldy bottle.

"Stop!" I swiped it from her. "Do not drink this!"

"Why you being so mean, Nukkun?" She climbed onto me, reaching for the bottle.

I screamed. "Not looking! Not looking!"

"It's mine!" Yakishio moaned.

There it is again! Right against my back! Yup, I feel it this time!

"Is someone in there? Marcooo!" A voice I recognized. It was our homeroom teacher, Amanatsu Konami.

"Sensei! We're here! Polo! Polo!" I shouted back.

There was a click, a rattle, and the door slid open. We were saved.

Amanatsu-sensei took a good long look at the sight before her. "Having fun, are we?"

Perhaps we were not saved. A half-naked Yakishio lay strewn on top of me. Perhaps we were simply out of the proverbial frying pan and into the literal fire.

"You two finish up first," Amanatsu-sensei said flatly.

"Wait, don't shut the door! I need your help!"

"I've been in some crazy scenarios in my time, but during class? Really, now?"

"TMI, Sensei, now please for the love of God help me!"

Once I'd managed to free myself from Yakishio's delirious grip, she went out like a light right on the floor.

Once more, for the record: I was not looking.

***

Oral rehydration solution: a magical liquid filled with electrolytes and glucose used to treat dehydration.

"God, OS-1 is so good," Yakishio sighed.

"It's hitting the spot."

Our nurse's office always kept some handy in case of idiots like us.

Amanatsu-sensei gave us a sour look, arms crossed. "Forget class. I want the both of you resting in here for now. You there. Boy. I'll let your teacher know. What's your name?"

"Nukumizu, and you are my teacher," I said. I'd long given up on her ever remembering.

"I am? That makes things easy," she said. "They're all yours, Konuki-chan."

The nurse waved as Amanatsu-sensei left, then she took a seat in front of us. Sexy nurses always struck me as something of an urban legend, but the only thing legendary about Konuki-sensei were her legs, which she made a show of crossing.

An impish grin played about her lips. "How are we feeling?" she asked.

"F-fine," I stuttered. Why couldn't she just be normal?

"More, please!" Yakishio held out her empty bottle. She still had a bit of a funky look in her eyes.

Nurse Konuki obliged. "Drink it slow, dear."

"Yippee!" Yakishio cheered, quickly starting on the new bottle with a doofy smile.

"Heat stroke is not to be taken lightly, you two," the nurse said, suddenly stern. "It can be life threatening, to say nothing of potential lasting symptoms."

"I understand," I said. "We're sorry."

"Good. I know what it's like to be young. Some things you just can't stop. Some passions just can't be smothered. And the harder you try, goodness, sometimes that makes it all the better. Right?"

"I'm... What?"

"It's okay. No need to explain." Konuki-sensei held a finger up to her lips and winked. "Whatever happened in that shed, that's between you and your teacher."

Communication was breaking down, and I didn't have the energy to repair it. So I changed the subject. "Do you and Amanatsu-sensei know each other?" I asked.

"We both graduated from this very school, as a matter of fact," Konuki-sensei answered.

"I guess that makes you both our senpai, technically. What was Amanatsu-senpai like as a student?"

"Oh, you'd never guess it now, but between you and me, she was a bit of an airhead. A total klutz." I was positively flabbergasted at this information. "We were regulars in this office. She always had some bump or scrape that needed seeing to." Konuki-sensei chuckled fondly. "And now here I am, working in that same room."

She swapped legs, crossing one nylon limb over the other, and looked up at the ceiling. Her gaze wasn't quite as distant as you'd expect from a bit of reminiscing.

"What are you looking at?" I asked.

"The stains on the ceiling. Some things never change," she sighed.

"You have a good memory."

She must have been a sickly kid. It was heartwarming, really, growing up to take a job in spite of her weakness. And at her alma mater too.

"Oh, I wouldn't say that," the nurse said. "I just got l—I laid on my back most of the time." I felt robbed. "Anywho, drink up and get some rest."

Sensei pulled back the privacy curtain and put Yakishio in bed before she could doze off sitting up. I downed the last of my OS-1, and she took the empty bottle.

"Rest," she said. "This sort of thing is worse on your body than it actually feels."

"Right. Thank you."

I let my head fall into the pillow. The stains on the ceiling leered down at me, evoking images of a young Konuki-sensei in our uniform. I yanked the blanket up over my head.

God, I wished she hadn't told me that.

***

The last chime of the bell echoed in my ears. I groggily turned over. I had no idea how long I'd slept for, but from all the noise outside I guessed it might have been lunchtime. Through a gap in the curtain, I spied Yakishio fast asleep in her bed. I debated going over and fixing the sheets to cover up her exposed belly but thought better of it.

"Wow, I do not want to eat," I muttered.

It hit me all at once. Wow, I did *not* want to eat. I had no appetite whatsoever. Sleeping through the break sounded much better. The cold comfort of the sheets against my cheek could not be denied.

Until Konuki-sensei threw open the curtain, that is.

"You have a visitor, Nukumizu-kun."

Yanami leaned out from behind her and waved.

"Yanami-san?" I said, still half asleep. "What are you doing here?"

"I heard you and Lemon-chan were here. Everything okay?" Yanami asked.

"Yeah. Fine." I sat up. "Yakishio-san's pretty zonked out."

Konuki-sensei shot me a suggestive look. "Yanami-san here's brought you lunch. Oh, to be young."

"Er, Sensei, whatever you're thinking, it's probably wrong," I said.

She nodded knowingly (she did not, however, know). "Don't you worry. I can take a hint. You've got the room, Yanami-san. I'm going to step out for a few."

"Oh, okay. Thank you!" Yanami called after her. "Hungry, Nukumizu-kun?" She held out a bag with a bento box inside.

"The door locks, by the way," Konuki-sensei said just before leaving. She wasn't even trying to hide the smirk on her lips.

Amanatsu-sensei was one thing, but how in the world was *she* allowed to be a teacher?

"The heck's that?" I said under my breath.

I noticed the glare of a lens deep within the clutter of books on the nurse's desk. It was a phone. A currently recording one. I went ahead and turned it off.

"What are you doing?" Yanami asked.

"Nothing," I said. "Let's eat."

We took seats across from each other. Yanami pulled out a large Tupperware container. Evidently, the era of cramming two portions into one bento box was over. Inside was a big yellow blob.

"Omurice?" I said.

"Yep, and I'm proud of how this one turned out. See how pretty it looks? I folded that baby perfect."

She stabbed a spoon into the middle and cut it in half. I waited, patiently wondering how exactly we were going to split this. Surely we wouldn't be taking turns with the same spoon. Surely she wasn't *that* crazy.

She handed me a spotless white plate. "Borrowed some stuff from home ec," she said. "Take it." I did. Yanami scooped out my portion and dumped it onto the dish rather gracelessly. "There. Manners—hands together. Let's eat."

I followed suit. "Th-thanks."

I couldn't remember the last time I'd had omurice. One bite was enough to bring me back. That was the flavor of childhood right there.

"Good, huh?" said Yanami. "What's the verdict?"

"I'll say...400 yen."

"Not bad, not bad." She nodded and took another bite. I felt that was a fair pricing. It was about what you could expect buying premade meals at the store. "Very mindful of you."

I was going to regret taking this bait. "What?"

"It's a delicate balance. You don't want to be rude, so you don't go too low, and you don't wanna come off as a cheapskate either. That pushes the price up. But going too high means less for you in the long term. That pushes the price down," Yanami explained. "S'just social dynamics." I had no words. She'd hit the bullseye, and judging from her pompous smirk, she knew it. "Where those lines intersect is where you got 400 from. Tell me I'm wrong."

She wasn't, and that was the worst part. Did she realize I was being generous? Did she even care?

"I've got a question for you," she went on. "Is 400 *really* what you meant? Listen to your heart, Nukumizu-kun. What does it tell you?"

She'd made a strong case. I couldn't lie anymore. "If you say so. Three hundred—"

"Nuh-nuh-no! Wrong direction!" Yanami sputtered. Her machinations were truly a mystery. "Sheesh, man. That's your problem right there, Nukumizu-kun."

That right where?

"Fine," she said. "I'll break 400 one way or another." *Thunk*. Yanami produced a thermos.

"Adding soup to up the value, huh?" I mused.

Naive. We lived in a world of surplus and competition. Soup came free with most lunch specials nowadays. Some cafés even threw in coffee and toast.

Yanami unscrewed the top and poured the contents onto the omurice. "Who said it was soup?"

"Béchamel sauce?" So that was why there hadn't been any ketchup. Personally, I was more of a ketchup guy, but points for fanciness. Taste dictated that I acknowledge that much. "Four hundred fif—"

I stopped myself. This was a slippery slope, and at the bottom lay a world of endless toppings and endless upcharges. Patience.

"Go on," Yanami said. "Finish the sentence."

I ignored her and tried a bite. "Holy...! This is awesome!"

"Heh," she chuckled. "Got that around New Year's. It's the good stuff. *Imperial Hotel.* So how much, huh? Look me in the eye and tell me that wasn't an *Imperial* experience!"

She had me. Imperial Hotel wasn't just any brand—it was top shelf stuff. I couldn't not appraise it accordingly. My pride as a man with taste was on the line, and I just knew that, should I disappoint, my palette would be ruthlessly put into question.

"500 yen..." I said.

"Thank ya kindly."

Yanami sneered. She must have felt so proud of herself for nailing me like that. I was in what we in the business liked to call "damage control mode."

There was a yawn and a swish of curtains. "What're you guys doing? Sounds like fun."

"Good morning, Lemon-chan," Yanami said. "Feeling better?"

"Better than better," Yakishio replied. "That nap was just what I needed."

"Oh, hey. I'm glad you're not..." I trailed off. Images resurfaced. The chaos in the shed. The sights.

Yakishio found a chair for herself, raising an eyebrow. "Hey, Nukkun, I don't actually remember much of what happened. Do you?"

"Who, me? Oh, totally! Amanatsu-sensei found us!" I shot off.

"I don't remember that at all. Guess she's the one who got me fresh clothes." She tugged at her gym uniform.

The tan lines.

"Yup! Uh-huh! It was all Amanatsu-sensei, and I *wasn't* looking! Didn't see a thing!"

"Uh, yeah, I'd hope so," Yakishio said. "Why would you?"

"Nukumizu-kun, you're being kinda gross," said Yanami.

The looks they gave me. They stung. I could hear the void calling.

"Anyway, what is that? It looks super yummy!" Yakishio said.

"Oh, it totally is," Yanami said. "Made it myself! Here, open up." She held out a bite for Yakishio, who graciously accepted.

"That *is* good! The sauce totally makes it. What even is it?"

"Imperial Hotel, and I know, right? You've got good taste. Unlike *some* people." Yanami gave me a smarmy glance as she held out another bite for Yakishio—from my plate. "There's plenty more where that came from."

"Excuse me." The door rattled open. "Is Lemon here?"

Ayano Mitsuki poked his head in, catching Yakishio mid-bite, mouth agape. He made a wry smile.

Yakishio shot upright. "Mitsuki?!" Her face turned from tawny to bright red.

"I heard you'd passed out from heat stroke," Ayano said. "Guess I worried a little too much."

"Nuh-uh! Oh, I'm feeling so faint. I'm so glad you're here to nurse me back to health!"

"Here." He held out a bag of fruit cups and apple sauce. "I'm guessing you have an appetite."

"You got all that for me?" Yakishio said.

"Maybe jumped the gun a bit. I don't know why I thought you'd be worse off."

"I am! I'm so sick I can hardly swallow! Thank you so much!"

"You might be right." Ayano reached for her cheek.

"M-Mitsuki?!"

He plucked a grain of rice from her face. "I'd have trouble eating from there too."

"I-I-I… Th-thank—"

"Anyway, I don't mean to be a bother," he said.

"D-do you wanna stay a while?" Yakishio spat out. "Yanami-san made omurice, and it's really good!"

"She did, huh?"

"Mitsuki-san. There you are." Another visitor appeared at the still-ajar door—Ayano's study buddy, Asagumo Chihaya.

"Oh, did you need me for something, Chihaya?" Ayano asked her.

"I was thinking of using the study rooms later, since we don't have lessons today. Would you like to join me?"

"Sorry, I've got to be home early today. I'll see you there tomorrow."

"Okay. I'll message you tonight." Asagumo promptly traipsed away.

Ayano smirked back at her. "So much for 'see you tomorrow,' I guess." There was something there. Something that definitely hadn't been when I went to cram school with those two. "I'm going back to class. Take it easy, okay, Lemon?"

"I-I will," Yakishio replied. "Thanks!" She watched Ayano leave with forlorn eyes. It was a textbook case of lovesickness.

"Hey." Yanami materialized next to me and jabbed me in the ribs. "What's with Miss Doe Eyes?"

I sighed. "She's got a crush on Ayano."

"Huh. Interesting pair."

"I went to the same junior high school as them, but I think they've been together since elementary."

"Which makes them," Yanami deduced, "childhood friends."

I didn't buy it and made that known on my face.

She shook her head. "You just don't get it, Nukumizu-kun. There are two types of women in this world: besties and bitches." Quite the dichotomy. Yanami scowled at me. "So which one is that other girl?"

"That was Asagumo-san," I said. "They met at cram school, third year of junior high if I remember right."

Yakishio, having finally come back down to planet Earth, slammed her hands down and leaned across the table. The dishes clattered. "What do you guys think she is to him?!"

"Personally," Yanami said, "I don't see how they could be anything but friends, given how little time they've known each other for."

"I knew it! I totally agree!" Yakishio shouted.

"Okay, come on. You guys saw the way they looked at each other," I interjected. The ensuing vitriol was incredible. Silent eyes threatened my very life. I shrank away. "I'm… I'm sorry?"

"So, what?" Yanami accused. "You think a year-long *fling* means more than a time-tested childhood bond? Is that what you're saying?"

Yakishio nodded. "What she said! Yanami-san gets it!"

Something about this felt disingenuous. Like a washed-up veteran giving dated advice to a newcomer.

"I feel a connection with you, Lemon-chan. The kind I can't really describe," Yanami said. "I'm rooting for you, girl."

"That means so much to me, Yanami-san!" said Yakishio. "I feel like I can take on the world now!"

And they lived happily ever after. Except for me.

"Yakishio-san, you're eating my lunch," I said.

"I am? It's pretty good. You should have some too."

"You're using my spoon."

"I mean, then take it." She held the spoon between her teeth, bobbing the handle up and down at me.

I reluctantly pried it from her. The warm, glistening, saliva-coated silver was almost… No. Not even a little. It was disgusting. I jammed it back into her mouth. She gurgled.

"I'm not that hungry anyway. You can have it," I said. I was never good with eating or drinking after people. A trait I often forgot about myself, because I never ate or drank with people much to begin with.

"Well, then I'd just feel bad. I can leave a little for you."

"A little." I'm honored.

"Oh, by the way, Nukumizu-kun," Yanami said through a mouthful of omurice. "Komari-chan told me to tell you to be at the club room after school. No excuses."

I wondered what for. Maybe the student council had found something new to get on the lit club about.

I let my eyes rest on the girls and their ricey, omelety feast. They were attractive, I had to give them that. The only fly in the ointment was, well, everything else about them. An odd kinship connected them. I could already tell that Yakishio had the makings of a loser, just like Yanami.

"Whew," Yakishio sighed, "that was good." Suddenly, I tasted metal, then egg, then sauce. My (admittedly extremely rude) train of thought was cut short by a spoonful of omurice. "See? Told ya I'd leave some." She shot up out of her chair. "I'mma head back. Tell the nurse I said thanks."

Did she have any notion of the concept of hygiene? You couldn't just go around shoving spit-covered spoons in people's mouths, especially when it was *your* spit. Being cute could excuse some things, but not that. Regardless, Yakishio left, escaping justice, and I was frozen stiff.

Yanami snickered. "Someone's blushing."

"A-am not!"

"So naughty, indirect kisses at school. The scandal!"

"I-I'm not blushing!" I lifted up my plate and started shoveling the last bit of the omurice into my mouth.

"Oh, by the way, I won't be able to make it to club," she said. "Going shopping with a friend."

"All right. Noted."

Wait a minute, she still planned on going to club? I would have been impressed even hearing she remembered what its name was.

"You won't be too lonely without me, will you? No crying, okay?"

She was laying it on thick. Would the teasing never end? I looked up, disgruntled, to see that she was genuinely frowning at me. Now I was just confused.

"I'll manage, thanks," I said.

"Phew." Yanami scooped up the last few grains of rice on her plate. "Hang in there. You'll be all right."

What in the world was I to this girl?

***

Tsukinoki-senpai looked at me, then at Komari. The air was heavy. Komari fiddled around with her fingers before quickly hiding them beneath the desk when she realized I was watching.

"We are gathered here today for one reason and one reason only," the vice president began. "A matter concerning the very existence of the literature club has presented itself." She theatrically raised two fingers, one on each hand. "I have unfortunate news and annoying news. Which do you want to hear first?"

"No good news?" I asked.

"I can give you the unnecessarily-and-tediously-verbose option if you like."

"Never mind. Let's have the unfortunate news first."

Tsukinoki-senpai nodded and lowered one of her fingers. "Our days of lazy reading are over. We are now authors."

"You weren't already writing things?" I said. "You're the lit club."

"We did," the vice prez said. "Once. Even released a periodical journal. One theoretical member of ours potentially won an award from MEXT too."

Wow, color me impressed.

"Why did you stop?" I asked.

"Do I really have to spell it out for you?" She clicked her tongue and wagged her remaining finger. "We *say* we will write, and then we don't."

Komari nodded enthusiastically. There was an in-joke I was clearly missing.

"Long story short," Senpai said, "the student council called us out at the club president meeting. They said we haven't been functioning as described in our activities."

"Well, I mean..."

"Which is strange, because I thought I did a pretty good job at hiding that little tidbit of our club."

A very scary student council lady came to mind. Uh-oh. It was time to change the subject.

"Why not start another journal?" I said.

"That would mean paying for paper, printing, and finding a way to distribute it. No, I have a better idea." Tsukinoki-senpai thrust out her phone. "Our pens shall leave their marks on the world wide web! On Bungou ni Narou!" Komari clapped her furious little hands. Senpai gestured for silence again. I suspected the audience was planted. "The important thing is that we upload *something*. It can be a short story, chapter one to something longer, whatever."

Narou was a popular self-publishing website. We wouldn't have to worry about paper, printing, *or* distribution.

"That takes us to the annoying news," she continued. I sat up straight. "In order to get the creative juices flowing, the lit club will be holding a field trip!"

"A *what*?" I said.

"A rec center in Tahara just so happened to have an opening in their lodge this weekend. I snagged us two rooms."

"Wait a minute, this weekend is *two days* from now."

"The publishing biz moves fast, baby. You rookies have a lot to learn if you wanna keep up with me!"

Komari started to clap again, thought a bit, and then tapped at her phone. She held it out. "I'd rather stay home," it read.

I was with her there.

Tsukinoki-senpai chuckled ominously. "Clearly the implications aren't apparent enough. See if you still feel that way after I mention..." she flashed a grin, her glasses gleaming, "canned goods."

Like tuna? Soup? Surely there was more to it than that. Maybe she was referencing a certain deadline-crazed author trapped in a hotel, but that felt flimsy at best. Also, literally, how was that relevant?

Komari got it, apparently. Her eyes sparkled. "Whoa..."

"Exciting, right?" said Senpai. "Doesn't it just get your blood pumping?"

"Yeah!" Komari cheered, nodding at mach speed. "Canned goods!"

Obviously, I had missed a memo somewhere.

"You can write on your phone or on paper, whatever you prefer," Senpai said. "The president will be bringing his laptop, so we'll make uploads from there."

"But none of us have even decided what to write about," I pointed out.

"We'll worry about that come the weekend. For now, everyone get brainstorming."

I had an idea or two rolling around in my head, but nothing I'd really developed into an actual plot ready to be put to paper. This was a tad sudden.

"Do you know what you're writing?" I asked.

"I mean, it's Bungou ni Narou. Probably some isekai." Surprisingly trendy of her. "The hook'll be Mishima gets isekai'd after committing harakiri, Dazai can't live without him and hurls himself into the Tamagawa Aqueduct."

Less trendy, but okay.

"Wait, that doesn't line up. Didn't Dazai die first, *then* Mishima?" I said.

"Don't like, don't read," Tsukinoki-senpai proclaimed. "Little details like that are trifling in the face of true love."

"Care to back that up, Komari-san?" I whispered.

She typed for a moment without offering me so much as a sidelong glance. "Yes. You don't get it. True literature is about the heart."

"In my universe, all you need to get over taking a hit from a Yamanote line train is a quick dip in a hot spring, so it's whatever," Senpai said. "Shame neither of you are eighteen yet, because boy is it gonna be spicy."

Was R-rated content going to fly for officially released club material?

"Bad… Family friendly, please."

Yeah, that's what I'm—

I nearly jumped out of my own skin. Standing in a shadowy corner of the room was Shikiya-san, second-year student council pencil pusher.

Tsukinoki-senpai gave her a quick glance, completely unfazed. "How long have *you* been there?"

"Dunno," Shikiya-san breathed. "Fell asleep. Waiting on people." Her head fell languidly to one side with her eyes fixed on me. "You have a proper club… Very good." She jotted something down (without looking again) then collapsed onto a chair. "Tsukinoki-senpai… Field trips require papers. Please submit them."

"Will do," Senpai said. "I'll herd the president over there by tomorrow."

"We are always watching…"

Would it hurt them to blink? Like, once? She was scaring Komari. Poor thing was shaking over in the opposite corner.

"Is it just me, or do you guys have it in for us?" Senpai griped.

"We are indiscriminate in our proceedings… Expenditures. Budgeting. Disbandment. Eradication…" Shikiya-san trailed off, and just like that, in grim silence, she shuffled away.

I still didn't know how to comprehend her existence. I doubted I ever would.

"Do you, uh… Do you guys know each other?" I asked Senpai.

"We have a bit of history," she replied. "Normally, she's a little more docile. Doesn't move a whole lot, that girl."

"Is she, like, okay?"

"She's got surprisingly good grades. Was in the top ten on the last test, apparently."

A gyaru(?) *and* a scholar? That was the perfect combo, as far as I was concerned. If only she weren't utterly terrifying.

"You seem pretty smart yourself," I said.

Komari rushed over and kicked my chair hard. "N-Nukumizu! We don't... We don't talk about Tsukinoki-senpai's grades!"

"Are they bad?" I stopped myself from commenting on the irony of her wearing glasses.

"I prefer the term 'brimming with potential,'" Senpai said. "Also, speak for yourself. You had a midterm recently, didn't you?"

"Uhhh, I think I ended up thirty-seventh in my grade."

Shocked silence filled the room. Did I look that dumb?

"I'm sensing a lack of potential," Tsukinoki-senpai said.

"It's very...middling," Komari added. "Be better."

Did I really deserve this?

"You could have had a steamy rivalry with the cool, bespectacled valedictorian," Senpai ranted, "or a red-blooded friendship with the confident and assertive class representative who 'helps' his bro out of a tight spot in his studies. There's just nothing to work with."

I didn't mind that.

"O-or at the very least," Komari chimed in, "you could be 222nd like Tsukinoki-senpai. Th-that could be something."

"Heh, what can I say?"

What was she so proud of? There were six classes of first-years of about thirty-eight students each, which put the total at...228.

"Don't you have college exams coming up?" I said.

"I'm well aware and not worried," she said. "I'm *very* decisive. Even got a first choice all picked out already."

"I'd be more concerned about whether they pick *you*."

The glasses and her pretty-girl demeanor had lowered my guard. Now, though, I could be certain. She was as crazy as the rest of them.

"Wh-what are we doing Saturday, Senpai?" Komari said.

The vice president quickly pulled out her phone. "Right. So we'll wanna head waaay south on Atsumi, get off at some point, and maybe take a bus. There'll probably be one."

Maybe you can check?

"All right, Aidai-Mae station sounds good." She beamed. "Be there at seven or eightish. And don't be late!"

She wasn't gonna check.

***

I took a detour by Toyohashi station on my way home. Seibunkan's flagship outlet was there, the city's largest bookstore and the best place for me to check up on releases.

Knowing that we'd be publishing our own original stuff on Bungou ni Narou, I had to make sure I was up to date on the latest trends. I'd already researched the trending tags and featured works online, but that was like fishing for a whale in open ocean. Physical media operated by different rules. Couldn't neglect good old-fashioned legwork.

I scanned the titles laid out for display. "Isekai, isekai, and more isekai..."

Some read like the setup to a joke. Others bordered on period piece. I picked up one book, then another, then another, studying the subtle nuances and thematic shifts. How fascinating it was to witness a genre evolve and establish its own quirks in real time.

"Seems like the play to me."

"M-move, Nukumizu." A small girl shoved me out of the way.

"Komari-san? What are you doing here?"

"R-research," she said. "I don't...know much about light novels. I came to st-study." She scanned the colorful mosaic of covers. "They're...getting pretty big these days."

"Yep. Most start out self-published online," I explained. "That's the current trend, anyway. They call that particular variety of fantasy isekai 'narou-kei' or 'narou-style.'"

"Th-that's the reincarnation stuff?"

"That's an element of it, yeah. Over the last decade we've seen some twists on it, though. Superpowers and slow-life elements are pretty much part and parcel nowadays, which may sound unrelated, but it's all connected by the same theme. It all comes back to folk who are burnt out on modern society and are looking for an escape."

"Wh-what's the theme?"

"Validation," I continued. "Making the reader feel invincible and the world feel like a welcoming place."

"Isn't that what...slice-of-life is for?" Komari asked.

"It can be, but it's missing the whole 'cheating the system' aspect. Because, well, most readers are only really going to experience retirement through characters who have what they don't. And they know that."

Komari grimaced. "B-being an adult sounds depressing..."

"Everything in the genre comes down to two basic fundamentals: glory through battle, and love and peace everywhere else. The only thing that changes between works is how those concepts are portrayed and balanced. What's interesting, though, is there's this whole subgenre of ostracized protagonists that's been splintering away from more female-oriented stories that center around doormat heroines and—"

"O-okay, I get it!" she interjected. "J-jeez, you could make a title out of that rant... What's the deal with those anyway?"

A reasonable question I had answered numerous times in my head.

"The title functions as a sort of neon sign for the reader, conveying what makes that particular book special. Like a tagline on a snack at the store, basically," I said. "That's why they all sound the same. They're all following the same general tenets."

"So, do...do you have a title all picked out, then?"

"Sure do. *Sage from Another World Aims for a Slow and Sustainable Lifestyle via Reincarnation Cheats!* Fits the format perfectly. My first goal'll be to place in the rankings, then—"

"I found it."

"You what?"

Well, damn. There it was. And it had five volumes already. That was a shame. The protagonist would have been on his sixth wife by then, if it were me.

Komari tried and failed to stifle her snickering. "A-after all that...and there's a book with the exact same title," she giggled.

I sulked to myself. "Well, what about you? Have *you* decided what you're writing?"

"Not isekai... Not really interested. I-I was thinking more something like this." She guided me to another section of the corner where romance and folk novels filled the shelves. I recognized a few that had movie adaptations. "I-I've actually been working on it for a while."

"For real?" Komari of all people had gotten the jump on me? "What, uh... What's the title?" I wasn't above pilfering an idea or two.

Komari waffled a few times before shyly showing me her phone. *"Ayakashi Café's Comfy Case Files."*

Sounded like something bordering on proper literature. Little more grounded, but still character-focused. This was, unfortunately, entirely not my field. I perused the shelves to get a better idea of the genre.

I grabbed one of the books. "Wait, this is literally your title."

"N-no!" Komari protested. "Look! That's case *record*. Mine's case *files*."

"And that makes it different?"

"Y-yes. It does." She puffed her chest out, her tiny body positively overflowing with certainty.

"Copyright infringement's on the table. Noted."

"Y-your title was worse."

"Pot meet kettle, Komari."

That set her off. She looked at me like I'd insulted her family. "'K-Komari'?! What happened to the '*-san*'?!"

"Oh, so you can call me Nukumizu all you want, but now I'm the bad guy? It's easier to say that way."

"I-I mean, I guess." Komari gripped the edge of her shirt. Always so difficult.

"I'm gonna get my books and leave," I said.

"W-w-wait!" she blurted. "I-is... Is Y-Yanami coming?"

"No? I came alone."

"N-not today, I mean! Is she, um, joining the lit club?"

"Dunno," I said. "She mentioned showing up, so she'll probably be there again. You worried she'll ghost us?"

I imagined she would have liked having another girl her age around.

"She... She's pretty..." Komari mumbled.

"True, but why's that got you worried?"

"Pretty girls...don't join the lit club."

Now that was outright slander. On behalf of all bookish girls in the world, I was offended.

"Oh, come on. Tsukinoki-senpai's plenty pretty," I said.

A dangerous thought occurred to me. There were only two girls in the lit club. I'd just complimented one. Oh god, how was I going to save this?

"Sh-she doesn't count. And I'm, w-well..."

"Hey, don't beat yourself up."

We sure were heading right where I knew we would. It was time to play *I Spy*.

I snuck a glimpse at her out of my periphery. Her trembling lips were certainly unremarkable, and her bangs were messy, and you could barely see her eyes through them, and what you *could* see was similarly unremarkable, but she was far from ugly.

"You've got plenty to work with," I said. "You shouldn't put yourself down like that."

Komari made a weird guttural sound at the back of her throat, and her bag fell to the floor. She leaped away from me several paces, face on fire.

She managed to squeak out, "H-hashtag Me Too..."

"What? Why?! I hardly even said anything!" I blubbered. "I wasn't trying to be weird, okay?"

How had one little half compliment gotten so quickly spun in the wrong direction? Komari kept glaring. A wave of exhaustion hit me. She *really* hated my guts.

"Look, I'm sorry," I said. "I shouldn't have said anything. Your appearance is your business."

"O-oh. Sure. That's that, then."

It was easy to forget I was doing this girl a *favor* by even involving myself with the lit club.

"I'll see what I can do about Yanami. Then you won't have to see me as much." I spun around and started to leave. I was so ready to get my crap and go home.

"Wha... Huh?! W-wait!"

Komari smacked me in the back of the head before I could get far.

"Ow! What's wrong with you?"

"I-I wasn't trying to...!" she sputtered. "I didn't mean...!" She stepped right up to me. I could almost see fumes puffing out of

her ears. What reason she had to be mad was anyone's guess. If anything, *I* deserved a tantrum or two. "Y-you better not ditch, o-or I'll...! I'll tell Senpai!"

"All right, all right, I get it. I'll be there tomorrow," I said.

Komari whipped out her phone and started furiously typing before shoving the screen in my face. "Not just tomorrow! Every day!"

"Every day?"

"Every day!" she spat, a little too literally. And without another word, she scurried away.

I was left utterly confused, dumbfounded, and flabbergasted. I wiped the droplets from my face. She really had to learn to say it, not spray it.

***

I didn't start on my way home until the sun was well on its way below the horizon, even with how long the days had gotten. Red tinged the sky, the buildings, and the streets, and that would soon give way to purple, which would quickly give way to night. This time of day was always the loneliest to me for some reason. I picked up the pace.

A girl in a familiar uniform appeared in front of me. Streaks of the setting sun illuminated Kaju's profile in deep orange. A plastic bag hung heavily from her fingers. I hurried forward on lighter feet and took the bag from her.

"Oniisama!" she yelped. "You scared me. Just now on your way home?"

"Yup. Late day for you too?"

"Mom and Dad said they wouldn't be home until after dark, so I got caught up in talking with a friend," Kaju said.

I peeked inside the bag. Udon noodles, onions, quail eggs, yams—all the ingredients for our family's favorite dish: Toyohashi-style curry udon.

I noticed my sister peering up at me. "What?"

"I found out today that I'll be away from home over the weekend. Is that okay?"

"Uh, sure. Why are you asking me?"

"I was worried you might get lonely. You won't cry, will you?."

Seriously, what was with everyone treating me like a sad little puppy all of a sudden? Where was that attention a week ago?

"I'll manage," I said. "Won't be home this weekend either. Going on an overnight field trip with the club I'm in."

"Wait, you are?!" Kaju hollered. "Are you telling me you have friends now?!"

"I dunno if I'd go *that* far..."

Kaju scampered off and flew into a nearby grocer. "Your finest adzuki beans, sir! We're having red rice tonight!"

"Well, hey there, Kaju-chan." The owner sauntered over, wiping his hands on his apron. Since when was she that popular? "Celebrating something?"

"Yes, sir! My brother's made his first friend!" Kaju proclaimed with glee. "Whoever they are, I need to whip them up something special!"

"That's just wonderful." He looked at me. "And you're the guy I've heard so much about? All of us business owners have been mighty worried about you."

I can never come here again.

"We were even thinking of making you a checkpoint for the big stamp rally," the owner said. "Guess we won't need to anymore."

Please, God, end this.

"My congratulations," the man went on. "Kaju-chan, go ahead and take some mochi while you're at it."

"Thank you, sir!" Kaju's eyes twinkled like stars. "So who are they, Oniisama? What are they like? Are they half as amazing as you are? Oh, I bet."

"I, uh..."

"Is it a girl?! Oh, goodness, I'm not ready. I'll need to plan meetings, set dates..."

"Listen, there's no friend," I interrupted. "I'm just going with some people in the literature club."

"You...haven't made any friends?"

"Um. No."

Things got uncomfortably quiet. A motion-detecting light went out, casting us in darkness.

"Make it soybeans, sir," Kaju said solemnly. "I'll boil them with some kombu at home."

"It sounds like you'll need the luck," the owner said real low. "I'll throw in some rolled barley."

Why was it starting to feel like I was attending my own funeral?

"I'll, uh, hang in there," I said.

"You do that, son," said the owner. "Don't be too hard on yourself."

That was the tone we left on. We were on our way back home.

"Still, a club? A field trip? That's all totally new for you," Kaju commented.

"First time I've done anything like it since I got forced into the Boy Scouts in fifth grade."

We didn't speak of that summer. Nightmare.

"Baby steps, Oniisama," said Kaju. "You're making progress."

"Maybe. Feels more like things are happening around me and I'm just along for the ride."

"That's fine too. Nothing wrong with seeing where it takes you, is there?" She grinned and patted me on the head. "I'm very proud of you, Oniisama. That's my big brother."

She then yoinked one of the bag loops from my hand.

"Feel like helping?" I said.

"Just feel like spoiling you a little today."

Kaju smiled brighter than the sunset. I couldn't help but smirk back, slowing my pace to match hers.

It didn't feel right letting my *little* sister spoil me. There was something...oxymoronic about it. Maybe I needed to do a little more than just "hang in there."

Current tab: 2,367 yen.

***

Literature Club Activity Report: Tsukinoki Koto—
Is It Painful to Be the Person Who Waits?
Or Is It More Painful to Be the Person Who Sleeps Alone?

The clicks and snaps of game pieces on a board echoed down the hallway. A man in military garb slid open the door and entered. There, on one side of a shogi board, sat a cross-legged man in loose, unkempt kimono robes. He simpered, a familiar expression, and felt his stubble.

The military man barked, "Why are you here?"

The man in the kimono regarded the intruder with surprise, then, upon recognizing the uniform, shook his head and returned to the game board. "Mishima-kun. We meet again." He picked up a piece and admired it, a melancholic calm gracing his visage. "My wish is granted. Here I am. Though the people...perplex me." *Clack*. The noise simply entertained the kimono man. "Our clothes. Our games. I've yet to find something they cannot replicate. The elves are a rather versatile people." A knowing glance at Mishima. "Especially their women." A smirk. *Clack*.

Mishima sat opposite him. "Do you have any idea what this is, Dazai-san?"

"A world beyond our own, yes, though not so different from Tsugaru. Wouldn't you say? Granted, a certain General Mori would delude himself otherwise."

"You've met?"

"More than met. He likes his pretty little blondies, doesn't he? Some proclivities never change, no matter the world." Dazai rattled a pair of shogi pieces in his hand amusedly.

"I won't play your games. What is the meaning of this? Why are you idling about here? You know he can give you a second chance."

"Did you come to see me, or did you come to chat about the general?" Dazai brought his bristly face next to Mishima's when the military man said nothing. "I heard what you did. Sliced your gut right open. Did it hurt?"

Mishima moved his king one space forward without heed. "I've never liked you, Dazai-san."

"And yet here you are. We both know how you really feel." Dazai pushed aside the shogi board and gripped the only game piece he truly cared to play with—Mishima's hand.

"Dazai-san, I—"

"I know you do."

With strength born seemingly from the ether of Dazai's sickly body, he toppled Mishima to the tatami, his chiseled physique at the mercy of

[The following contents redacted by discretion of the club president.]

***

Friday. The classroom was buzzing more than usual. Friends greeted friends, sharing weekend plans, figuring out who was free to hang out with who. Phones made that particular social dance a little easier, but there was something intangibly important to the tangible, to talking face-to-face. Humans were social creatures, complete with all the limitations therein.

I leaned my elbows on my desk, hands clasped together. "Speaking of freedom..."

To be truly free was to be alone. Like yours truly. I didn't have a dance to dance, plans to share, obligations to get in the way of my carefully concocted weekend.

Until recently, that is.

Since our oh-so reliable Tsukinoki-senpai couldn't be trusted with it, I had spent the better part of my evening last night working out train and bus schedules for the field trip tomorrow. I also checked out some popular sightseeing spots but *only* out of curiosity. I was already looking stuff up anyway. Nothing to read into.

"Morning, Nukkun!"

"Huh? O-oh. Morning?" I stammered. Yakishio Lemon plopped down at the desk in front of me. Something wasn't computing in my head. "Can I...help you? What's going on?"

"Uh, nothing? It's morning, so, you know. Good morning." It was morning. She wasn't wrong. But since when were we close enough to exchange greetings? Yakishio didn't elaborate. "So hey, I remembered that thing in the shed yesterday." She leaned her head thoughtfully to one side. "I was thinking today—"

"Y-you remember?!" I blurted. How in God's name was she so composed? "I wasn't looking, for the record! Not even a little!"

I *did*, however, remember the way it felt. The softness. The springiness against my back. The...everythingness. I couldn't look her in the eye.

"Ya lost me, dude," Yakishio said. "I'm talking about the books."

"The books?"

"You're the one who told me to tell him to come pick 'em up! Still fuzzy for you or something?"

"Oh. No. Yeah, I remember that. That sure did happen. It's all you."

"Cool! We'll be there after school!" Yakishio casually waved as she trotted off to her seat.

The tension drained away before immediately coming back, because that was when I noticed all the eyes on me. Mostly male eyes. Jealous, angry eyes. All of a sudden, everyone wanted a piece of the poor background character, and I didn't even know why.

"...So like, what the hell's that about?"

A few hours later, Yanami and I were sitting on the fire escape stairs.

"Lemon-chan's got admirers," she said, digging out a lunch basket. "And, well, you guys were getting all friendly."

"Admirers? Huh. Admirers." Admirers, huh? "Wait, who's got admirers?"

"Lemon-chan, cotton ears. Do you need to see the nurse again?"

Yakishio? Admirers? Literally how? She was cute, granted, but did anyone know her on any level other than skin-deep?

"She's pretty and fun to talk to," Yanami went on. "I mean, okay, yeah, she can be a bit, *y'know*, and how she even managed to pass the exam to enroll here is one of Tsuwabuki's seven wonders, but that stuff aside." She nodded matter-of-factly. "She's pretty and fun to talk to."

Pretty and fun to talk to were powerful traits, for sure. I was convinced.

I inspected today's lunch. The basket was packed with onigiri, sausages, karaage, broccoli, and various finger foods with toothpicks for easy eating. And easy sharing, at that.

"Why wasn't this the first thing we tried?" I said.

"Yeah, Anna, come on," she muttered curiously. "Could've been so easy."

"Agreed."

I went for one of the onigiri. A paper bento box, a half-mochi rice glob, and the remnants of ravaged omurice flashed before my eyes. So many stupid solutions to an easy problem. Albeit the omurice was an entirely unrelated matter.

"Anyway, so you're going on an overnight trip? That sounds fun."

"We'll see," I said. I took a big bite. "The only bullet point I've been told is 'canned goods.'" I felt a crunch, stopped chewing, and looked down at the rice ball. Q-chan pickles, a Mikawa regional specialty.

"You're only staying the night, right?" Yanami asked. "Are Tsukinoki-senpai and Komari-chan the only girls?"

"Yeah. Guys are me and Prez Tamaki."

Yanami pulled out her phone and started swiping. "Looks like there's a beach nearby. Cool. Wonder if I can get away with last year's swimsuit."

"What do you mean 'last year's'? Do they expire?"

Also, wait, was she going?

"To be fair, it's not like I need a new one *every* year," she said, "but who doesn't like new swimsuits?"

"Sure, I guess. Didn't you literally just buy one though?"

"I—what? No?" Yanami cringed hard and scooched away. "Literally what are you talking about? You're being creepy, Nukumizu-kun. Like, it's kinda gross."

Gross and *creepy. A new record...*

"But you did," I argued. "You literally had to buy one for school."

"Oh. Oh, that's what you meant!" She unscrunched her nose then shook her head. "No one wears their school swimsuit to the beach, are you kidding me? I'd honestly rather go in my underwear."

"It can't be that bad."

By her logic, the education system was subjecting its students to cruel and unusual punishment every day.

"It literally is," she asserted. "Also, don't ever do that again. Ever. You're lucky I realized what you meant, but even still. That was almost cancelable levels of creepy."

I was three-for-three on the insults. I changed the subject before we hit four. "You know this trip'll take up your entire weekend, right? Don't have any plans already?"

"That's just the thing." Yanami's eyes became cast in shadow. "So I ran into my auntie the other day..."

"Who?"

"Oh, Sousuke's mom. We've been friends a long time, so our families are close." I prepared myself for more nonsense. "Anyway, she asked me why I haven't been coming by in the mornings." She chuckled exactly twice at herself. "Which is funny, y'know, 'cause like, why would I? He's got a girlfriend. It'd just be weird for me to keep waking him up."

"R-right."

"And *then* she asked if we were fighting. We did used to do that a lot. Get in little arguments over stupid things." Yanami watched a passing cloud float by. "Wish it was that simple."

I had no idea how to respond to any of this.

"So apparently my parents had the same idea, because turns out they're planning a friggin' surprise barbecue together. Totally out of nowhere!" She got right up in my face. "I need you to take me away from here! Take me to the ocean, Nukumizu-kun!"

This was sounding a little too much like a cheesy soap opera.

"Isn't there a much easier way to achieve the same effect?" I said. "Can't you just step out while it's going on?"

"You haven't seen my dad at a barbecue, okay? That man will grill for hours and hours until I get home!"

"Uh, okay, then plan a sleepover with some friends?"

"And *not* talk relationships? Listen, Nukumizu-kun, that just doesn't happen, and unlike you, I actually care about what my friends think of me!"

First of all, that was plain rude. Second, I had no friends. I racked my brain for a way out, any escape whatsoever.

Yanami wasn't having it and gave me an unamused look. "You sure are bending over backward to keep me from coming."

"Not on purpose," I insisted. "It's just, can't you tell the situation to one of your buddies and have *them* bail you out?"

"I mean..." Yanami frowned. "It's hard to explain. I don't want them caught up in all the drama."

"Oh. You haven't told anyone? Even a little?"

"I can't, really. Everyone kind of already knows, and they're trying to keep things feeling normal. I don't wanna be the one to make things heavy." She let her eyes fall a little. "I can read the room sometimes, thank you."

"Not with me, apparently."

"Well who else am I gonna vent about all this with?" she grumbled.

"O-oh. Um..." She'd said something similar to me a few days ago. I dug for my phone. I knew when to throw in the towel. "I'll have to ask to be sure. You're technically not a member and all."

"I can be! I'll do it right now, even!" Yanami blurted. "Send me Tsukinoki-senpai's ID. I'll talk to her."

"I, uh... I know Senpai's from the group chat we're in, but I don't have yours."

Yanami stared blankly at me. "Just check the class chat, dude."

Duh, of course, I'll just—

"I don't have that."

"Huh?" There were no words for an uncomfortable length of time. Yanami fled from the tension by staring down at her phone. "I, uh... Huh. Sorry, this is...awkward." She blinked and darted her eyes around. "But hey, like, that's just you, y'know? Classic Nukumizu-kun. Doing his own thing. Right?"

That was the saddest attempt at consolation I'd ever seen.

"It's fine. Doesn't bother me. I've only just recently started using LINE anyway," I said.

"Y-yup! Classic Nukumizu-kun!" she repeated, a little more affected this time. "Here, add me. Do you know how?"

"Yeah, I got it. It's that 'shake it' thing."

Tsukinoki-senpai had done all the behind-the-scenes of getting me in the club group, but I made sure to do my research. I was a veritable friend-adding pro.

"The what thing? There's no 'shake it' thing."

"There's not?"

Then where the heck had it gone? Did someone lose it?

"Just show me your QR code," she said.

Where do I...?

Yanami reached over and tapped a couple of things. "There. You should've gotten my friend request. Now you accept it."

"Okay. Done. And now you're added?"

"Yep. You can add me to the lit club group chat now."

I slowly navigated my way through the menus, and when I was done, Yanami nodded in proud approval.

"Back to Lemon-chan," she said, counting what remained of the karaage with a toothpick, "when'd you two get all buddy-buddy?"

"Do we look like buddies?"

"I mean, she gave you a nickname."

Nukkun, she'd taken to calling me. It came out for some reason in her heatstroke-related delirium back at the shed, and evidently it stuck. Surprisingly irrelevant in the story of how we knew each other.

"Remember the guy who showed up in the nurse's office?" I said. "Ayano Mitsuki, from class D."

"Oh, right, the guy Lemon-chan was making eyes at. He was pretty handsome."

"The lit club has some books he wants to borrow. Yakishio-san's kind of acting as the go-between."

Yanami hummed in mild interest, then tossed a piece of karaage and broccoli into her mouth. "I can start calling you Nukkun too, if you want."

But why?

"Fifty yen a day," she added. A shrewd twinkle sparkled in her eyes.

I looked away. "No thanks."

Kaju's questionable friends may have been on to something.

***

Fifth period came and went. I was killing time until the next bell, wandering the hallways away from all the people.

One more period, and then we'd have to go over all the weekend plans in the club room. Ayano and Yakishio were coming at some point too. Things were busy. Long gone were the peaceful doldrums of yesterweek.

I stepped outside. There was a water fountain next to the athletics field where students fresh off PE class usually thronged to. Not today though. I turned on the faucet, feeling like a king. Today was pool day, and I was in heaven. It was the perfect distance from the classroom. Its outdoor location bestowed upon it a kind of holy distinction from other, less pilgrimage-requiring water fountains. And hey, there was a charm to that rustic taste.

I stood back up and wiped my mouth—just in time to meet eyes with a familiar someone doing the exact same thing.

"N-Nukumizu," Komari Chika grumbled from the opposite fountain. She was not happy to see me. "What are you doing here?"

"Quenching my thirst," I said.

Komari eyed me suspiciously. "A-all the way out here?" She was too sharp for her own good.

"I could say the same to you. You're trying to get away from the classroom too. Going on your own water fountain crawl."

"Wh-who asked you? I-I did my research, I'll have you know."

Intriguing. My inner scholar chuckled ever so condescendingly. She knew not who she was talking to.

"Oh, my dear Komari," I said. "I, too, am particular about my water. Admittedly, I am curious as to your findings."

"O-oh really?" She narrowed her eyes at me. "Wh-which fountain did you use this m-morning?"

The Tap Water War had begun.

"Around first and second period, you'll find the one on the fourth floor next to the third-year classroom, on the east end, is of superior quality."

"Your r-reasoning?"

"The water that early will have been sitting in the tank overnight. This goes for all water in the building, but that spot in particular will be lower in chlorine and still somewhat cool in the summer sun. It's the best water on the fourth floor, bar none."

Komari hummed with interest.

"The closer you are to the tank, the better," I continued. "The one trade-off is you'll have more chlorinated water. That location is the exception. It offers maximum freshness with minimal drawbacks."

I ran my hand through my hair like the savant I was. My victory was assured.

It should have been.

Komari scoffed. "S-so naive."

"What? How so?"

"E-east side of the fourth floor is best i-in the afternoon. Just before lunch."

Before lunch? That was madness. The upper floors were suboptimal that late in the day.

"Explain yourself," I demanded. "The chlorine content is higher. The water is warmer. What benefit is there?"

"N-naive. So naive. The higher temperature m-makes it easier on the stomach." Komari wore her victory on her expression. The tables were turned.

"B-but the chlorine!" I objected. "It's too bitter! The smell!"

"E-exactly. It dulls the senses."

"The senses?"

What reason would she have for "dulling her senses" just before lunch? And then it hit me.

"I-it makes it...easier to eat in the bathroom."

There it was. How I wish I could have unheard it.

"You have a whole club room!"

"W-we're not allowed to use it during lunch," she said. "People were using it to sk-skip class."

Here was sloth in its worst form. The indolence of one had led to the tragedy of another.

"Look, Komari, how about you come to my spot?" She made a gagging noise. Lovely. "Hey, I'm not inviting you to eat with me. There's a set of stairs to a fire escape around the old annex. Pretty deserted. You can take a different floor or something."

"I-I'll consider it." She hurried off. I didn't even get a passing glance.

For all her quirks, I was maybe starting to think she was warming up to me. At least compared to when we'd first met. She was talking to me more without her phone, and that was something.

Right. Class.

I jogged back inside.

***

It was after school, at the club room. Ayano Mitsuki grabbed the last of the Abe Kobo volumes.

"They're impressive works," he said. "I don't know where to start."

Tsukinoki-senpai crossed her arms haughtily. She was in a good mood. The lit club had found a new member in Yanami *and* had two new visitors. "Start wherever you like. They're all yours to borrow."

"Have you read all these, Senpai?" Ayano ran his fingers along the many spines lining the shelf.

"Only *The Woman in the Dunes* and *The Box Man*, unfortunately. I dropped *The Wall* around the beginning of *The Crime of S. Karma*."

"So the very start of the book," Ayano laughed. I wasn't convinced it had been a joke. He picked one of the volumes. "I'll go with the twelfth collection for now."

Yakishio peered over his shoulder. "How're you gonna tell who's who 'n stuff, Mitsuki? Shouldn't you start at volume one?" she asked, completely unironically.

"Hm? Oh, I'll be able to tell," he replied. "It's not all one story."

"So not like *One Piece*."

"Not quite. This particular volume just happens to have a few works I'm particularly interested in."

That guy had Yakishio down to a science. Whatever was going on between him and Asagumo, those two made a surprisingly decent pair.

I turned to Yanami, who was off on her own wearing a goofy paper crown with "New Member" scrawled across it. She munched on some Pocky, humming to herself. At least she was easy to entertain.

"Say, Ayano-kun," Tsukinoki-senpai began ominously, "how do you feel about our little club here?"

"I have to admit, it's comfortable," Ayano said. "But I'm already so busy with lessons at cram school. I'm afraid I wouldn't be around very often at all."

"Why, that's perfectly fine! Pop in whenever you like, steal a few books, leave, whatever you need to do. Nukumizu-kun will handle the formalities. You just consider these shelves your own. In fact"—her glasses gleamed—"we've got connections with the library. Let's just say certain strings can be pulled to get you what you need."

"Wait, seriously?"

"I'm a woman of my word."

Ayano looked over the recruitment flier with interest. The vice prez had made an impressive case. "I'll consider your offer."

"Your cute girlfriend there's free to join too," she added, setting her sights on Yakishio. Aggressive, this one.

"Wha—me? I-I'm the girlfriend? Oh gosh, oh jeez, I dunno what to say." Yakishio floundered bashfully. She took the flyer quite readily. "I'm already on the track team though, so, y'know."

"Not a problem," Senpai continued. "In fact, you'd fit right in! We're all doubled up, as a matter of fact." Was I in *another* club without realizing it? That was news to me. "Say you're not feeling it one day, just can't get those legs moving. That's where we come in. Throw our president under the bus. Tell the track team he's forcing you to come in, and boom, you've got an excuse to ditch!" Tsukinoki-senpai sneered. This was what people meant when they said not to talk to strangers. "C'mon, it'll be fun. School's better when it's fun, yeah? Nothing wrong with having options. And you get to see your boyfriend more. That'll make him happy."

Yakishio lit up like a Christmas tree. "It will? It'll make Mitsuki happy?" She made no effort to deny the obvious.

Ayano laughed softly, stowing the book in his bag. "I can't put that kind of pressure on her. We're not even dating."

"Oh, was I mistaken?" said Senpai.

"She's got way better options than me. She's always been popular." He swung his bag over his shoulder. "Thank you for the book. I'll be back again when I'm not—"

Yakishio suddenly nabbed his shirt. "I'm not seeing anyone, though! And I wouldn't go out with just anybody!"

Ayano blinked at her. "O-oh." A sun-kissed face blinked back at him. "Sorry, I...didn't mean to imply anything."

"No, it's okay. I-I didn't... Sorry."

Tsukinoki-senpai glanced between them for a while. "Are you sure you're not dating? You definitely look like it to me."

She was surprisingly dense—and bad at keeping thoughts to herself.

"C-c-come on, Senpai, you heard Mitsuki!" Yakishio said, grinning all flustered.

"Right," said Ayano. "And I already have a girlfriend."

Yakishio froze solid in an instant. It was like a bomb went off.

"Um, guys? Is everyone okay?" Ayano said.

The door clicked open. "H-hello." Komari took one look at the state of affairs inside, and the door clicked back closed.

"D-did I put my foot in my mouth again, Lemon?" Ayano asked.

"Y-you—you have a...girlfriend now?" Yakishio came back to life like a robot on half-dead batteries. "S-since when?"

"Just recently, actually. I guess I never told you, did I? I'll introduce you soon. Promise." He scratched at his cheek shyly, then lowered his head. "Excuse me, I didn't mean to ramble. I'll go ahead and excuse myself."

"Hold on," I spoke up. "Is it Asagumo-san?"

"That obvious, huh? I'll introduce you too before long." Ayano smiled in his charismatic way before turning back to Yakishio. "Ready to go?"

"Go?" Yakishio parroted.

"You said you wanted my help shopping. I've still got time until my lesson."

The man had only innocence in his expression. There was no malice. Only densely packed neutrons in that head of his.

"Something, er, just came up earlier. And I was sorta thinking I might join the club, so I-I'mma stick around here."

"Yeah? All right, then I should get out of your hair. I'll see you later." He bowed one last time, and then he was gone.

We were left to pick up the pieces, and boy were there many. The silence went on for what felt like an eternity, until Yakishio finally started to crumble. I hurriedly shoved a chair beneath her, stopping her from hitting the ground at the last second. She held her hand out to me.

"Uh, what?" I asked.

"Gimme one of those sign-up sheets." I did. She scribbled her name, rambling under her breath. "Girlfriend... He's got a girlfriend... Mitsuki has a girlfriend... Ha. Ha ha. Boy, do I look stupid."

Just a little, I thought to myself.

Yanami unceremoniously plopped the "New Member" crown from her head to Yakishio's. "You, uh... You did good."

"It sure doesn't feel like it." Yakishio wrapped her arms around Yanami's waist and buried her face in her stomach.

I dragged Tsukinoki-senpai out of the room before the sobbing could start.

She threw a few timid glances at the door. "Hey, um, so, was that my fault? Just now?"

"Yes. Extremely." I pulled out my phone, sighing. "About tomorrow. I looked up the bus and train schedules. I'll send the details in the group chat later. Still meeting at Aidai-Mae?"

"Er, yeah, but hey—"

"Make sure you send a complete list of what everyone needs to bring well in advance. Also, I haven't been able to get in touch with the president. Can you make sure everything's good on his end?"

"Nukumizu-kun, is now really the time for this?"

I gave her a look. "Who's the one who royally screwed everything up?"

She flinched. "You don't mince words, do you?"

Something told me I wouldn't get far with her otherwise.

"I'll handle things here, so you can—" I spotted a figure peeking out from a wall down the hallway. Komari was still feeling out the mood. "Go check on Komari actually, please."

"Can do. That's my specialty."

Senpai whipped toward Komari, hands out and fingers wiggling. Komari booked it. Senpai gave chase.

Times like these were why some loners were hermits by choice—specifically to avoid crap like this. It was always something.

I leaned my back against the wall and zoned out at my phone. A message came from Yanami. She was asking if I wanted to stop and grab something on the way home. No idea why she'd thought to invite me. I was about to turn her down when another message came that made me do a double take.

They were going to a very special dive, far away from school—the family restaurant Yanami'd had her heart torn out at just days prior.

***

"Come in! Sit wherever you like!"

The person at the counter greeted us as we entered. It was the same old family restaurant I was used to, just a twenty-minute walk from school, in the next town over.

Yanami plopped down in the booth and patted the seat next to her. "C'mere, Lemon-chan. You sit here."

"Thanks." Yakishio did so uncharacteristically quietly. I couldn't help wondering if maybe she'd have had a better chance with Ayano if this were her default setting. "Never heard of this place, Yana-chan."

"It's nice, right? No Tsuwabuki students or anything. It's a bit of a hole in the wall."

Yanami went straight to scanning the dessert menu. I eyed her. Wasn't this where Hakamada Sousuke had broken her heart? What sort of person used that same place as a getaway for their friend who'd *also* just had their heart broken? The mental fortitude on display was insane to me.

"Not gonna order anything?" she asked me.

"I mean, you do know this is..."

"This is what?" She cocked her head.

"N-never mind," I said. "For the record, I'm not picking up the bill for you this time."

"I know that. What kinda girl do you take me for?" She pushed the button to signal a waiter. "Bit insensitive to talk about money at a time like this, I think. Don't you worry, Lemon-chan. It's on us."

Yanami accusing someone of being insensitive. How ironic. Also, it didn't escape my notice that she'd used "us" in that sentence.

"Yeah, sure." I surrendered. "She and I'll split your bill, Yakishio-san."

"But you don't have to do that," Yakishio said.

"Consider it a welcome gift. You're the lit club's newest member, so don't worry about it."

"You let us treat you today, okay?" Yanami paused and looked up. "Wait, didn't I just join too?"

"We'll do you later," I said. "Excuse me, we're ready to order!"

I struggled to believe Yanami would have the self-control to indulge responsibly. Case in point: She hadn't looked at anything but the dessert menu and *still* ordered a Salisbury steak.

"Medium-size rice, please," she added.

"You not gonna have dinner at home, Yanami-san?"

"Nothing ruins a diet faster than dessert before dinner. Don't you know that?"

So dinner before dinner is fine, then? The logic checked out.

Yakishio pointed to something on the dessert menu. "I'll have a Black Thunder parfait."

"Ohmigosh, okay, I need that after my entrée!" Yanami blurted out. So much for the diet.

"Large fries and three drink cups," I ordered. "Again, I ain't paying for you this time. Just so we're clear." I could not stress that enough.

"I know that," Yanami pouted. "I'm serious, Nukumizu-kun—that right there's why you have no friends."

The girls got up to fill their cups. I watched them leave. It was business as usual with Yanami, which was a relief, if a little confusing.

An hour went by. An hour of gripes, complaints, and struggles, and of Yanami stuffing her face with Salisbury steak. Yakishio was smiling more near the end of it, though, so that was good. We'd gotten somewhere at least.

"You can wait outside, Yakishio-san," I said as we took a spot in line at the register. "We'll take care of the bill real quick."

Yanami raised an eyebrow at me. "So you *can* be nice."

"I'm not a robot. When a failgirl's in need..."

"A what?"

Oh, crap. I'd let my filter down and stuck my foot in my mouth. Not good.

"I...ail...gir..."

"You said 'failsomething.'" Yanami studied me, trying to read my face. "What was it? C'mon, I'm dying here."

I turned away a full ninety degrees like an animatronic. "No, I said al... Al...Gore. Like the guy."

"Who's that? Friend of yours?"

Not likely.

"He's a famous politician. In America," I said.

"Where did *that* come from?"

A fantastic question. I glanced around, desperate for a lifeline, and spotted a poster. "American Burger Fair." Thank the gods.

Yanami followed my gaze and planted her fist in her palm. "Oooh, I get it. You wanna get burgers next time. Yeah, that'd be fun!"

I wasn't getting out of treating her now, but that was a small price to pay for smoothing over that little slip of the tongue. Pick your battles and all that.

My turn came at the register. I handed the cashier our receipt.

"Oh, I forgot," Yanami said. "We never set a price for today's lunch."

"Oh yeah. Let's call it 500 yen. It was pretty good."

"Nice!" She put her hands together excitedly. "I'll take it!"

The tab was sitting at 2,367 yen, minus 500 put us at 1,867. Side note: The bill for here ended up being a healthy amount higher than that, all together.

"Hope you've got money, 'cause I'm all out of credit," I said.

"I heard you the first time," Yanami griped. "Like I keep saying, that's your problem right there. Oh, I have a T-Point card."

I put my money in the tray. "That's me and half of Yakishio-san."

"Gotcha, so that leaves..." She popped open her wallet and instantly froze.

"What?"

I swear to God if she's broke again. Surely she wasn't. Surely she had more than two brain cells to rub together behind those pitiful eyes of hers. She started to tremble. It wasn't looking good.

"No..."

Yanami looked up and met my eyes. Tiny, wet orbs welled in hers. "Nukumizu-kun. I dunno how to tell you this."

I could see them. Behind the tears. Two lonely brain cells working overtime.

I quietly pulled out a bill.

Current tab: 2,867 yen.

Too Many Losing Heroines!

INTERMISSION

A Hands-On Lesson in Passion

<"OKAY, COME ON. YOU GUYS SAW THE WAY THEY looked at each other.">

Only the harsh fluorescents above illuminated the dark nurse's office. Konuki Sayo made a note of something, voices playing through her earbuds.

<"I feel a connection with you, Lemon-chan. The kind I can't really describe. I'm rooting for you, girl.">

<"That means so much to me, Yanami-san! I feel like I can take on the world now!">

She circled Nukumizu's name in the center of the page and drew a line connecting Yanami and Yakishio's.

"Quite the triangle."

The video recording had been a bust, but her audio equipment had gone unnoticed.

She pondered the conversation. The girls sounded friendly, despite what their complicated relationship would imply. Though parts of the dialogue baffled the nurse, it was clear that there was no aggression between the rivals. This led to two possibilities, which Konuki noted down: Nukumizu and Yakishio were getting off on the thrill of going behind Yanami's back, or Yanami was in on it and the relationship was open.

Konuki twirled her pen and added one more: Yanami was aware of the infidelity but was actually into it.

She shuddered. *My, this is too much, even for me!*

For how average that Nukumizu boy looked, he had quite the system in place. In Konuki's time, two-timing (sometimes even three-timing) more often than not ended in metaphorical bloodshed. High school was awfully early to be learning concepts as advanced as these.

"I'm getting old."

The air conditioning hummed to life. Konuki leaned back in her chair and looked up, thinking back on times long gone.

Something crackled outside, like feet hitting dirt. At any other time, she would have thought nothing of it, but it was late at night. Konuki stood, flipping the switch in her mind into teacher mode. No student had any business being there at this hour.

She squinted into the darkness, out at the athletics field. A girl was crouched on the track, ready to fly, then she bolted forward so fast she nearly blended into the night. Konuki almost forgot to scold her. She threw on some slip-ons and hurried outside.

"You there," she said. "What are you doing out here this late?" It was then that she realized just how much of a coincidence this was. "You. I remember you."

"Oh, Sensei. You're still here?" The girl didn't sugarcoat her own surprise. "On a Friday night?"

"Adults are busy." Typically not with listening to questionably obtained audio, but she kept that to herself. "And I could ask you the same thing. It's after nine, young lady."

"Just had the itch to run. The team was off today, so didn't get a chance." She took a sports drink out of her bag and chugged it.

"Well, off you go. You should be home. Do you need me to walk with you?"

"Can I just do one more sprint? A quick hundred meters. That's all."

Konuki gave a lopsided smile. "Haven't had enough?"

The girl smiled back. "I'm feeling it this time." She stared across the pitch-dark track, eyes fixed on the finish line. Sweat dripped off her face. "This is gonna be the one. I can feel it."

Konuki found herself picturing a different childhood. Maybe if she had been a little more like this girl, things could have been different. "All right," the nurse said. "Go. Run." Not that she had any regrets. "And don't look back."

The young, tawny girl just had this way about her.

"Never do!"

Too Many Losing Heroines!

LOSS 3

Komari Chika Wins the Battle, Loses the War

A VIRTUALLY CLOUDLESS SKY GREETED THE FIRST day of the trip. We'd had a dry rainy season this year, to the point that I kind of forgot we were even *in* the rainy season.

One train and a bus later, the literature club had arrived at Shiroya Beach, just a short way from where we'd be staying the night. Shuffling and hopping around on burning hot sand, I laid out our tarp. I was the very picture of a fish out of water.

"Not bad, Nukumizu. Not bad at all." President Tamaki stabbed an umbrella into the sand. Hadn't seen much of him, but I was grateful for his rare attendance. Otherwise it would have been just me and four girls.

"I don't follow," I said.

"Yanami and Yakishio. You snagged us some real cuties." He looked longingly toward the changing rooms. "And just in time for the beach."

"Right, sorry about Yanami-san just kind of—"

The prez snatched my hand and shook it up and down. "I seriously owe you one, man!"

"You, er, really like swimming, huh?"

"No, man, it's the *swimsuits*! Think about it. How many men in this world can brag about having seen *four* clubmates stripped down at the same time?"

"I'm classmates with two of them," I said. "I've seen them during swim class at school plenty of times."

"That's entirely different. School-issue swimsuits and personal ones are completely separate beasts."

As far as designs and amount of skin went, I was with him. He seemed to notice he wasn't quite getting through to me.

"Look, girls wear school swimsuits because they have to," he began. The logic tracked so far. "They wear their *own* swimsuits because they want to. Get it? Do you see the difference?"

"Go on." He'd earned my interest.

"Shoulders and thighs are big no-nos normally, yeah? It's embarrassing to show them off. One exposed midriff and suddenly you're a slut. But the beach? It's no holds barred. You can flaunt yourself in what's basically underwear and it's totally socially acceptable." President Tamaki clenched his fist and turned his gaze skyward. "We are free to look, and they are free to be watched. It would be a *disservice* to avert our gazes! Maybe. Probably not, actually."

The man made sense. I was starting to believe in the magic of summer.

"You're right," I admitted. "I was blind to the truth."

"Oh?"

"Just one thought I had."

"Lay it on me," he said.

"You said they wear school swimsuits because 'they have to,' right?"

"That I did."

"In other words, they're being forced, in a sense, to expose themselves," I said. "I think there's something to be said for that."

"I see. Your perspective certainly adds a bit of spice to what would otherwise be a boring old PE class." The prez nodded. "One might even be able to put oneself in the shoes of an isekai protagonist, browsing the selection of beastwomen at a slave auction. I like the way you think."

"Okay, I wouldn't go that far." I was no longer part of this conversation.

"Interesting chat. Mind if I join in?" Tsukinoki-senpai appeared and yanked the president's ear.

"Owowow!" he yiped. "Wait a minute. Koto, where's your bikini?"

Tsukinoki-senpai tugged harder. The president howled. She had on a black one-piece with sheer fabric covering the chest area.

"Less horndogging, more swimming." She marched off, dragging Prez with her by his ear.

"Oooh, a parasol! Thanks, Nukumizu-kun."

I turned. "Yanami-san—"

I wanted to comment on the shaved ice she'd somehow gotten from god knows where, but her perfect skin flash-banged me before I could. There was so much of it. Her bikini was plain—plainly defective. I could have sworn those things were meant to cover more than what it did. She had a figure that defied her appetite, and…other things that didn't. "Last year's" swimsuit was maybe getting a little small.

Did it look good on her? Irrelevant. A foolish question. The only way I could describe my feelings at that moment was "gratitude."

"What's up? My bod got you buggin' out or something?" Yanami teased.

"I-I dunno," I stammered. "W-wasn't really looking." A pathetic attempt at maintaining composure.

Yanami planted herself in the shade of the parasol, satisfied. "You go ahead. I'm gonna eat first."

"Aww, you gotta come with, Yana-chan!" Yakishio came running next, carrying a beach ball under her arm. She stared out across the ocean. "Look how pretty the water is!"

She wore a tube top bikini, the kind without any shoulder straps. As if the tan lines weren't enough, the front of her top piece was held together by mere string at the cleavage. And yes, a lot was visible. More gratitude for the fashion designers of the world. I wondered if they had an Amazon wishlist or something.

"C'mon, Nukkun, you too!" she urged.

"I'm gonna watch our stuff," I said. "You go ahead. Yanami-san's gonna be at it a while."

Yanami shot me a narrow look. "Is that a challenge?" Before I could tell her that it was not, in fact, a challenge, she had scarfed the entire cup of shaved ice. "Done!"

"Already?"

"Naive Nukumizu-kun. Shaved ice is technically a beverage, don't you kn*waaagh*!" Yanami held her head in her hands and squealed.

"That's why we don't wolf down cold food, kids," I said.

Yakishio came over. "You okay, Yana-chan?"

"Feels like my head's about to pop..." Yanami sniffled.

I was starting to think that girl might not be the brightest bulb of the bunch.

"You run off once you feel better," I said. "I'll just chill here."

"Thanks," said Yanami. "I'm better, so I'mma go now."

"Don't take too long!" Yakishio shouted back at me.

The two hurried off, kicking up sand behind them. Yakishio hurled the beach ball at the president the moment he was within range. Had they even met before?

Meanwhile, I watched from afar. Something was nagging at me in the back of my mind. It felt like we were forgetting something.

That something kicked me in the back. "Wh-what're you gawking at, Nukumizu?"

Komari the Forgotten scowled through her hoodie. She took a seat a good distance away from me.

"Not gonna join the others?" I asked.

"D-don't feel like it."

The president looked over the moon with the girls all to himself. He was truly living his best life. Where had they gotten that orca floaty from?

Komari looked on with that same disgruntled scowl.

"I imagine the president'd like having you over there too."

"I'm f-fine." She started fiddling with her phone in a protective Ziploc bag and didn't look back up. "Wh-what about you? Don't you have a thing for Y-Yanami?"

"What? Why would I?"

The thought hadn't even crossed my mind. She was still hung up on that Hakamada guy for one thing, and it had barely been a week since she got rejected.

"Y-you're always together," Komari said.

"It just looks that way because you only see her when she's with me." Assumptions were the fate of every guy and girl who hung out together, apparently. We didn't even talk in class, like, at all, and Yakishio was our sole mutual acquaintance. "We've only just met, and there are circumstances. If that's enough to catch feelings, then I'm no better than those guys who imagine their whole future with a girl just because she said 'hi' to him."

Komari pulled her hoodie tight around herself and scooched away.

"I'm saying I'm *not* that." Mid-eyeroll, I caught a glimpse of what she had on beneath the jacket. "Is that your school swimsuit?"

"I-I didn't have time to buy one." She eyed me up and down. "You were p-probably in a rush too."

I laughed. "Please. This is last year's. Bit lame, but it works."

"I-it still has the tag on."

I panicked and started frisking myself. Komari smirked at me.

"Yeah, yeah, you got me," I confessed, clenching my fists. "So sue me. I was a little excited about going to the beach with some girls."

Komari, being one of said girls, spared no sympathy in her expression. "W-we swim at school."

"It's not the same. Do *you* get excited about gym class? No. It's not for fun."

"Okay, th-then humor me. S-say you were having 'f-fun' with some friends." Komari took one look at me and knew she'd already lost me. "S-say you were *paying* some f-friends to have fun with you." Cold, harsh reality, my old friend. "They a-ask you what you want to do. Do...do you play volleyball?"

"Nope," I answered without hesitation.

"Do you play in the w-water?"

She was right. I wouldn't normally be itching to do those things. She had missed one crucial detail, however.

"You're omitting something, Komari."

Yanami and the others were clambering over the orca floaty. Yakishio made a bold attempt to stand and drank seawater. There were shouts, and laughs, and chaos.

"I-I am?" she said.

"The 'friends' are girls, and they're in swimsuits." For a second, reality stopped feeling quite so cold and harsh. "Yeah, I think I would do those things." I shot up to my feet.

Komari gave me a blank, incredulous look for a second. "Th-then go on and get outta here!"

***

I lay on the hot sand, arms spread, and closed my eyes. Today was a day I would never forget. The day I went to the beach with a bunch of girls—and had fun. With that, I could live out the rest of my solitary days in peace.

Something cold touched my forehead. Yanami was handing out drinks in paper cups to everyone.

"Gotta stay hydrated, guys," she said. "So what're we doing about lunch?"

She split a pair of disposable chopsticks. My eyes fell to the yakisoba resting on her lap that she had implicitly deemed *not* lunch.

Tsukinoki-senpai looked around at us while she tied her hair back up. "Any ideas? We can pick something up and bring it back."

Yanami's hand shot up. "Yakisoba!"

It did smell pretty good. I was getting the craving.

"You're literally eating yakisoba right now," I said.

"Nah, this was a bust. I settled for somewhere less crowded and paid for it." She slurped up some noodles. "The one down there. That's a winner. I can feel it."

I should have known she'd be more than willing to go for seconds.

Yakishio tossed the towel she was drying off with to the side and stood up. "I'll go grab us some grub, then."

"Appreciated. Nukumizu, help her out, would you?" the president asked. He glanced around warily. "You can never be too careful. A fair maiden alone is just asking for a pickup artist scene to trigger. You know what they say: The best treatment is prevention."

"You are aware we live in the third dimension, right?" I said. Better safe than sorry, I supposed.

Yakishio and I set off across the sand. Walking next to a girl in a bikini was a little outside my comfort zone, but I wasn't complaining.

God, what am I, a little kid?

"Things went pretty late last night," I spoke up. "You make it home okay?"

"Yup, no prob," she said. "I usually take a few detours after practice anyway, so it wasn't much later than usual for me."

Silence. Dumb me forgot yesterday was still pretty fresh for her. Not the best topic for conversation. God, I was bad at this.

Yakishio peeked at me out of the corner of her eye. "Thinking about yesterday?"

"Just afraid I might've opened up fresh wounds, is all," I confessed. "Sorry if I, er, brought the mood down."

"I'll be real," she said. "Am I still sad about it? Yeah. Pretty sad. I could break down in like, two seconds if I felt like it. But why would I, y'know? There's always time to cry. I can do that when I'm not out trying to have a good time." She smiled an unconvincing smile and kicked up some sand. "I swear. Dude's denser than a brick, and suddenly he's got a girlfriend."

"He's a handsome guy. Smart too."

"I know, right? And he's fun to talk to, and nice, and..." Her shoulders dropped. "All those years we've been together, and I was never even an option, was I?"

"Uh, well, maybe. But I'm sure he meant well."

Yakishio looked at me. "You're not good at this, are you?"

I was not.

"Well, uh... Let's just have fun, yeah?"

"I can get behind that." She stopped, turned to me, and flashed a toothy grin. She snickered.

"Wh-what?"

Out of nowhere, she snatched my hand. "Let's run the rest of the way!"

Oh god, I'm not—

And run we did. Yakishio clung tight, leaving me no choice but to try and keep up.

"W-wait! Hold on!" I hollered.

She was fast. Insanely. Felt like she'd pull my arm out of its socket. It didn't take long for me to trip over myself and promptly face-plant into the sand. Yakishio tumbled down with me.

"Dude, Nukkun, how slow can you be?" she said. "What are you, a snail?"

"I'm not too slow. You're too fast!" I hoisted myself up, sand coating my body.

Yakishio made no effort to move. She flopped flat on her back and started cackling. "How does that even happen?!" She held her stomach and cackled some more. "We barely moved, and you're *covered*!"

"What does how far we went have to do with anything?!"

What did I do to deserve this? I tried to wipe the sand off my face with my arm but only caked it in even more.

"Stop! I can't breathe!" Yakishio wheezed. I continued to battle with the sand. "Oh, man. Man, my stomach hurts." She wiped a tear from her eye.

"Can we just go get lunch, Yakishio-san?"

"Forget the honorifics. Don't gotta be so formal." She held her arms out to me from the ground. "Yo."

"What? There a bug or something?"

She blinked at me a few times before picking herself up. "Yana-chan was right. You've got problems."

"Huh? What are you talking about?"

Yakishio prodded me in the chest. "Look, sometimes girls just wanna be girls. That's all."

"Huh. Noted," I said. Good to know.

She stared at me for a bit, then grumbled, "That right there. She was so right."

That right where?!

***

"Hey, guys! We got the food!"

"Careful, Yakishio! Quit all the flailing or you're gonna drop it!"

We returned, covered in sand with yakisoba in hand. From the good place—the one "down there."

"We're starving to death over here!" Yanami eagerly took them off our hands. The previous yakisoba was nowhere to be seen. Leave it to Yanami Anna to put to question the very existence of food comas. I knew she wouldn't disappoint. As she passed out the food, I noticed her sneakily keeping the largest helping for herself.

"Not eating, Komari?" I asked.

She was poking and fidgeting with the sand. Her food went untouched. "P-Prez is...reading my novel."

Were we finally acting like a literature club? I split a pair of chopsticks with my teeth.

The president took his yakisoba and finally looked up from the phone. "Just finished. Very well put together and pretty entertaining. Whaddya say we upload the final copy tonight?"

"O-okay." Komari's lips made a crooked smile.

"You've got a good, what, seven-k words here give or take? Let's split that into three parts while we polish it up."

"W-we have to split it up?"

"An average chapter'll be about two, maybe three thousand words. That's a nice bite-sized chunk that'll appeal to most readers. You'll need the title and blurb too."

I listened while I slurped on my yakisoba. The aroma was sharp and stung my nostrils just right. Yanami hadn't been kidding. This place was a winner.

"B-but it has a title."

"And it's not a bad one, but what do you think about adding a subtitle to it to sell it better?" the prez said.

A bit of a narou-style twist on Komari's original title. Interesting.

But man, I couldn't get enough of that yakisoba. The noodles were insane. They weren't store-bought—I could tell that much. Did they have them handmade? They must have.

I glanced at Yanami. She gave a thumbs-up. She knew.

"H-how do I make a subtitle?" Komari asked.

"So, for example, if your title were *Beach Time with the Lit Club*...what would you go with, Nukumizu?"

"Huh? Me?" I mumbled through noodles. I'd hardly been paying attention. I was all in on this yakisoba. Had to play it safe. There were girls here. "Maybe *And Then There Were None*?"

A boring answer but one the president seemed satisfied with. "Not bad if you're going for a mystery vibe. Referencing a more popular work could help readership too."

"Wh-what would...you use?" Komari said.

"Ah, yes, well, I might be partial to *But It's a Nude Beach?!* Or maybe *And the More You Strip the Higher Your Score!* In my professional opinion, that'd bump your numbers up by—"

Tsukinoki-senpai chopped the president square in the back of the head. "Thank you for your opinion, Shintarou."

"K-Koto..." he groaned. "I wasn't *actually* asking you to strip."

"Thank. You. For. Your. Opinion," Tsukinoki-senpai enunciated.

Someone get these two a room.

"The lit club gets up to some complicated stuff, huh, Yana-chan?" Yakishio said, digging through her yakisoba.

"Uh-huh," said Yanami. "Hey, did yours come with any meat?"

"I've got squid, but no *actual* meat."

"Man, I want meat."

"Same."

Four eyes and a brain cell for each. They were a dangerous duo.

Komari stared down at her phone, muttering to herself, "D-do they have to strip?"

"It was just an example. Your characters don't have to get naked," I said.

"A-are *you* getting n-naked?"

Why?

"I'm not getting naked. No one's getting naked. Eat your yakisoba."

***

The after-lunch lethargy didn't last long.

"Hey, they're doing an event or something over there," Yakishio said, leaping to her feet. "Let's check it out."

"Wonder if there're any vendors," Yanami mumbled between bites of her post-meal grilled corn. She didn't wait for an answer and stood right up. Her stomach knew no bounds.

Speaking of her stomach, when I looked up it was right in my face. "Y-Yanami-san, maybe throw something on first?"

I held out a jacket. She looked at it, then at me. "Why? I'm good. Just put sunscreen on."

"I'm not...talking about your skin." I looked away.

Yakisoba times two plus corn equals: big, protruding belly.

Yanami snatched the jacket from me, then hurled it at my face. "I-I'll wear my own clothes, thanks! I swear, you never learn!"

She grabbed her own hoodie, shoved her arms through the sleeves, and then marched off in a huff, corn still in hand, of course.

Yakishio started after her before turning back and grinning at Komari. "C'mon, you too! You've been sitting there all day."

Komari made a weird yelp and looked up from her phone just long enough to act flustered, then got to furiously typing something. The president put a hand on her. "P-Prez?!" she sputtered.

"Go on," he said. "Might be helpful for your novel."

"I-if you...think so."

"It'll be good for you. Koto, mind going with her?"

"Roger," Tsukinoki-senpai replied. "Let's go, Komari-chan."

She and Komari took each other's hands and trailed behind the other two. Prez and I hung back.

"We not going? I thought the best treatment was prevention," I said.

"Koto can handle it," Tamaki said. "If shooting people down were a sport, she'd be a marksman." Was that a compliment? I couldn't tell. He pulled out his phone. "Also gotta get ready to upload our stuff tonight."

"Right. Canned goods."

I was feeling the pressure of a looming deadline and hadn't written zip. I scanned through my notes for ideas but was soon interrupted by a DM. The president had sent me a text file.

"What is this?" I asked.

"Bet you're dying to know what Komari-chan wrote, hm?" He gave me a sly look.

I opened the file.

Literature Club Activity Report:
Komari Chika—Ayakashi Café's Comfy Case Files

Mizuhara Yuri, a first-year high school student, was on her way home one day, when she spotted a curious little creature.

"A fox?" she wondered aloud.

What struck her in particular was the animal's fur. Silvery and with an almost metallic sheen, it was. Yuri was stricken by its beauty and couldn't help but chase after it.

However, she quickly lost her way, finding herself in unfamiliar streets and, eventually, a quaint café, ivy suffocating its outer walls. Yuri felt drawn to it and so opened the door.

"Excuse me," she said, "can someone tell me where I am?"

A man stood inside—a man in chef's attire and of tall stature.

His long, silvery ponytail whipped behind him when he turned in surprise to face the visitor.

"Well, you're a persistent one," the man said to her. "Sit, and I'll brew you a cup of tea."

"I just want to know where I am, sir," the girl insisted.

"Why, you're in Between, and I'm afraid there's no leaving this town on an empty stomach."

While Yuri processed this information, another young man appeared, this time donned in the gentlemanly garb of a waiter.

"A visitor. How rare. Please, sit." The newcomer introduced himself as Sumire, and his smile captivated Yuri. "Welcome to our little retreat in Between."

Yuri still remembered her first visit like it was yesterday. She looked over the café from her usual spot—the table by the window. The owner, whom she heard referred to only as "Young Master," was scarcely present, perhaps only two days out of the week. That left only Sumire-san to look after things, though he never seemed shorthanded. They rarely had customers other than her.

Yuri took a whiff of her chamomile tea, a calming aroma, when a man suddenly entered. About him was an aura decidedly otherworldly.

The color left Sumire-san's face. "Sir!"

"I have come as was agreed," the stranger said. "You will serve me one dish."

"I-I'm terribly sorry, sir, but Young Master is out at present," Sumire-san pleaded.

"Then into the Between you will disappear."

Sumire-san looked to Yuri with desperate, unsteady eyes. "Oh, please, Yuri! You have to help us, or I'll be rendered into nothing along with this very café! You must cook for him!"

"What? But I can't cook!" Yuri exclaimed. "Can't you?"

"Not with fire. Not me," he admitted sorrowfully.

Yuri hadn't cooked much at all, much less for another person. She recalled the omurice she had once made with her mother and, to the best of her memory, attempted to recreate the dish.

The man scooped up a spoonful and scrutinized it. He took a bite. Then a second. He did not seem impressed.

The stranger placed the spoon down, shaking his head. "When next I visit, I expect better." And then he whisked himself out the door, leaving half of the omurice on his plate.

"You're incredible, Yuri!" Sumire-san cheered. "He never takes more than a single taste!"

Behind him suddenly appeared the owner. "I see my father's whipped up a storm in here."

"Young Master!"

He took a taste of the remaining omurice. "Unrefined," Young Master said. The spoon clattered as he set it down. "But not inedible."

"Cook it yourself next time if you can do so much better!" Yuri protested. "Is this how you treat all your customers?"

"I see. So the problem is you're a customer. We'll just have to fix that. You start tomorrow."

"I-I never agreed to—"

The man with the silvery hair backed Yuri up against the wall.

"Who was it that chased me to the ends of reality? I believe that makes you a stalker."

"I wasn't chasing you. It was a silver—"

He took her by the chin. "Call me Getsuko. Has a much better ring to it than 'Young Master,'" he whispered in her ear. "Though you'll get a taste for both in time. Quite thoroughly."

I see.

I looked up from my phone and stared at a passing thundercloud.

"I see," I said, out loud this time. It was admittedly beyond my expertise but an easy read. Credit where it was due, I couldn't put it down.

"She's good, huh?" President Tamaki grinned proudly. "She's a talented writer, that Komari-chan."

"Well, she's better than me at least." The petty side of me couldn't admit it without the self-deprecating twist.

"It's nice having you newbies around. We don't have to worry about the club so much anymore."

Cheers went up over where the event was happening. President Tamaki faced that way.

"So what are you writing?" I asked.

"Me? I've been uploading on Narou for at least three years now."

"Wait, really? Can I see your work?"

"Boy, way to put me on the spot." He made a show of reluctance while he fished for his phone. The title seemed familiar—*The Slave Girl I Found Turned out to Be an S-Rank Adventurer So Now She Calls the Shots.*

As a matter of fact, it was more than familiar.

"Wait, I know this. I've literally been following this," I said.

"No kidding? Wow. First time meeting a reader."

Many self-published authors online were students—that part didn't surprise me. What surprised me was knowing our club president was *Tarosuke-sensei*. The guy had over twenty thousand points on that one series.

"That's insane. You think it'll get published?"

"Nah, that's a long way off," he said. "There's plenty further in line than me." It was crazy to me that something with thousands of readers couldn't make the cut. I took his word for it. "I'll send you Yanami-san's later. How's your project coming?"

"I've got a gist of the plot but nothing on paper yet. It's like I get cold feet as soon as I try to actually write something."

"Then let's focus on the title and blurb. The important thing's that you write *something*, even if it's just one sentence."

I nodded. Couldn't argue with someone who'd written hundreds of thousands of words more than me.

"What do you think of the outline I sent you last night?" I asked. "I was thinking it'd make a good first chapter and I could get started tonight."

"Right, I did have a comment. The heroine needs a little bit more."

"More of a reason for her relationship with the protagonist?" I considered his advice. The main duo *could* have used a little more interaction.

"The opposite, actually," the president said. "The reason you gave is because the protagonist rescues her, right?"

"Right. The idea's that she starts off kinda thorny until the main character finally gets through to her with his kindness."

"That's bull."

I waited for a punchline that never came. "Huh?"

"What you've described is a business deal. The hero saves the heroine, so she falls for him. Love's not conditional like that. Love's not about favors." There was no humor on the president's face. "Love happens the same way water flows downhill. Infatuation is a switch that flips on and off. The heroine can't be infatuated. She has to *respect* the protagonist, genuinely admire him for who he is. No strings attached. It has to flow like water." He gazed wistfully up at the sky. "Wish I could get isekai'd and get the kind of attention those guys do. Think I'd have a chance if I got drunk and took a dip?"

"Maybe if you wait till Obon. I hear isekai's all the rage around that season."

I hadn't pegged him for a griper, not when he had the looks, the personality, and the pretty childhood friend most men dreamed of having. The grass was always greener somewhere else.

We chatted about nothing for a while until the girls came back, hauling a bunch of new luggage.

"We're back!" Yakishio called out. "And we brought souvenirs!" She carried a whole bunch of fireworks in her arms.

"Whoa, you guys buy all that?" I said.

Yakishio handed them to me with a smug grin. "You wouldn't believe it! I was all *zoom*! And it was like *nyoom*! And then *boom*, and I took the flag, and then they gave 'em to us!"

Tsukinoki-senpai heard the dial-up sounds in my head and took pity. "She won them at a Beach Flags contest. You should've seen her go."

"I-it was pretty cool." Komari nodded enthusiastically.

"D'aww, shucks, you're making me blush." Yakishio wiggled and squirmed like a bashful worm. "But don't stop, though."

One stick in the mud stood out among the high-running emotions.

"You okay, Yanami-san? You look upset," I said.

"There were no vendors..." Yanami eyed a beachside stall in the distance, hungrily, her lips mouthing the word "takoyaki" over and over.

"You're not gonna have room for dinner if you keep stuffing your face."

"Huh? Why not?"

This was not a question I was prepared to answer. Yanami waited patiently, and I could only ponder it myself. Why *wouldn't* she have room for dinner? Did philosophy have an answer?

"Speaking of dinner," I said, "we have to cook for ourselves at the lodge, right? What're we having?"

Yanami laughed at the foolishness that dared inspire such a question. "Don't you worry that pretty little meat-starved head of yours, Nukumizu-kun. Because *I* reserved a camping spot in advance. We're having a barbecue, baby."

"Oh. Okay."

I chose to ignore the irony of her having come here specifically to avoid a barbecue. Personally, I'd been hoping for curry. Rice in a mess tin just hit different.

"Whaddya mean 'oh okay'?" Yanami accused. "You got wax in your ears? I said we're having a *barbecue*! You know what a barbecue is? It's got meat, Nukumizu-kun! What more could a person ask for?" She backed off suddenly and put her hands together. "Oh, wait, I get the issue. Don't worry. We're responsible high schoolers." She gave a thumbs-up. "There'll be beef."

"Are...high school and beef related somehow?" I asked.

"Uhhh, duh. Everyone knows you can't have beef until you're in high school."

"No. That's not a thing."

"Huh? But my dad said..." The reality set in for me. I didn't like where this was going. "Was it a law? Or did the school say so?"

"It was probably his work or something. You know, like how some people only buy Toyotas for brand loyalty."

Phew. I'd saved it. No further down that road.

"Maybe." She hung her head thoughtfully. The ride wasn't over yet. "What does he do again?"

"I mean, he, er, probably does *something*, right?"

"Y-yeah! He does...something. He's always going on about how he's 'no sheep,' though."

This could not continue. The lore was getting too deep, and I wasn't equipped to handle where it would inevitably lead.

***

The bus wasn't too far off. If we wanted to have time to shower and change before it got here, we'd have to start packing up soon. Luckily, Yanami was on her last takoyaki.

Yakishio watched the waves hit the shore, stretching, while the rest of us cleaned up. "Hey, y'know what? Komari-chan hasn't been in the water yet."

"I, er—" Komari rifled through her bag for her phone. Yakishio cracked a villainous grin and took the chance to sweep her off her feet—princess carried. She squawked.

"Be right back!"

No one stopped her. We waved Yakishio and her victim goodbye as she darted toward the water. Komari's flails were in vain. That girl was a hulk.

"I'll get the parasol," I said.

"Return that to the counter with the floaty while you're at it," the president said. "I'll get our things together."

There was a splash, followed by a high-pitched screech. A surprisingly feminine one, coming from Komari.

"Shintarou, the other girls and I are gonna get off early to go shopping. You guys get our stuff to the rooms, if that's okay." Tsukinoki-senpai untied her hair. Dark locks fell onto her bare shoulders. She scrunched all the moisture out with a towel and got right up against the president to get a look at the bus schedule in his hands. "Plenty of time until the next arrival for us to get what we need, looks like."

"Move your hair, Koto. It's cold," the president griped.

"Get over it."

More flirting. *Would be a shame if, say, a meteor were to fall from the sky and blow them to smithereens. Sure hope that doesn't happen.*

"Bluh… I'm soaked." Komari came trudging back, wringing out her hoodie. Against the backdrop of the ocean, her form-fitting school swimsuit was especially striking.

This, I realized, was what Yanami had been talking about. The mismatch. The incongruity of rules and freedom. It evoked a cocktail of emotions born from secondhand embarrassment and immorality. This was high level stuff.

Yakishio brushed her hair back and put an arm around Komari's shoulder. "How was it? Felt good, huh?"

"A-all I taste is salt."

"Yeah, I bet! Isn't it the best?"

"A-all I taste is salt!"

"The ocean's salty. Didn't you know that? You say the weirdest things sometimes, Komari-chan." Yakishio grinned from ear to ear. Komari was fighting a losing battle.

Tsukinoki-senpai clapped her hands. "All right, enough goofing around, everyone! Time to get cleaned off and head to the lodge!"

I'd had my fill and honestly wasn't opposed to calling it a trip well traveled then and there.

I shelved the thought and grabbed the parasol.

***

The sun was on its way out, and with it the heat of day. Weird, unfamiliar cries from unknown bugs were giving me the heebie-jeebies.

"I'm putting the washed veggies here."

"Thankies. Set the chopped stuff out on that tray there, please."

Yanami had, for whatever reason, volunteered for cooking duty and, for whatever reason, singled me out as her sous-chef. You would assume that meant she'd have the skills to back it up. You would assume she worked that knife like a pro—but she didn't. She peeled that carrot exceptionally averagely. Occasionally leaning a little toward the left end of the bell curve.

"Did you have something to talk about, or...?"

"No, not really," replied Yanami. "Here, cut these carrots into circles. You know how to do that?"

I didn't grace her question with an answer. She and I got to chopping. Neither was winning any culinary competitions.

"Can't help wondering why you picked me instead of Yakishio."

Yanami froze. "Question. Have you ever been in the same group as her in home ec?"

"No?"

"Ah. Well." Yanami got extremely distant all of a sudden. "Let's just say some people don't belong anywhere near a kitchen."

My imagination went wild. What had she done? Ostensibly, she was a keeper. An athletics superstar. But it would seem that, deep down, a darker truth lurked.

"You know she's on fire duty," I said.

"Nope. None of my business."

They'd be fine, I was sure.

I remembered something I'd meant to talk about. "By the way, I read the story you wrote."

"Oh, already? Yikes, that's a little embarrassing."

"It was good. An easy read."

Hers was a short story. Just a cute little snippet about a girl on her way to school. It was a stream-of-consciousness sort of thing centered around her working up the nerve to say hi to a boy she liked.

"Gotta say, I didn't know convenience store karaage skewers were made like that," I said.

"Right? Most people don't."

Wait, what was the story about again?

I couldn't recall and didn't much care to. Yanami seemed happy enough.

She and I brought our prepped veggies over to the booths where the campsite kept the grills. The president was busy fanning some red-hot coals with Tsukinoki-senpai close at hand fanning the president, but one person was missing.

"Where's Yakishio?" I asked.

"I think that's her sulking over there," said Yanami.

There she was, just outside of the lamplight, her face black with soot, hugging her knees while she picked beans from their pods. Environmental storytelling at its finest.

"She looks busy," I said.

"Agreed."

***

Beef. Beef. Pepper. Beef. Sausage. Nothing could assuage Yanami's hunger. She was a meat-starved machine of gluttony. Not even my own slowly browning meats were safe from her talons, and all I'd had was cabbage, a bit of onion, and some corn at that point.

"Hey, I was working on that! It's not even cooked through!" I protested.

"Oh, whatever. You're so prissy." Yanami consumed the slice, caring little for the actual blood still dripping off it.

Some liked their meat well done, some liked them not done at all, and there could be no peace between these factions. Surrendering this battle, I settled for a charred piece of carrot while I eavesdropped on the others.

Reddish juices trickled out of the side of Yakishio's upturned lips. "Oh my *god*, this meat's good! Where's it from? Mexico?"

"Shintarou," Tsukinoki-senpai said. "This one's done. Plate."

"Th-this slice is done too!" Komari interjected.

"Thanks. Man, nothin' like the outdoors to make a good meal great." President Tamaki looked awfully content in the center of his mini-harem. I couldn't decide if I envied him or not. "You eating, Nukumizu? You gotta try this meat, man."

"I'll, uh, try," I said.

Something felt wrong. I was in danger and didn't know why. As I scanned my clubmates, a question occurred to me: How were they *all* engorged on meat already?

Yanami clicked a pair of tongs and laid out some more on the grill. "The texture makes me think Argentina, Lemon-chan. No one does meat like the Americas."

"Wow, you're like, a genius," Yakishio said. "Where's Argentina again? I know it's super far away. Maybe they dry-age their beef." She swallowed another cut.

Tsukinoki-senpai shook her head. "You want dry-aged beef? Come with us again next year. I'll show you dry-aged beef."

Wasn't she a third-year? How was she planning on being around next year?

Komari chewed on a piece herself. "I-it's been...a long time since I had beef."

They were devouring the slices Yanami had put on the grill mere moments ago. That settled it. I *was* in danger. I was surrounded by Team Rare.

I refused to go down without a fight and went for a cut of meat I knew would be fine raw, or close to it at least. After only a few seconds on the grill, I snatched up some sausage.

"Nukkun, you just put that down," Yakishio said. "Maybe let it cook first?"

"S-so impatient," Komari grumbled.

What? Why? What was happening? Had I slipped into a parallel universe where these people *weren't* literally just eating raw meat? The hypocrisy on display petrified me to my core.

Yanami held out some meat with her tongs. "He's probably just hungry. Here. This just finished."

I pulled my plate away from the dripping, barely-browned pork. Déjà vu.

Tsukinoki-senpai offered a plate. "Here, maybe this'll fill you up."

Onigiri. And the rice was red.

"Where'd we get that?" I asked.

"Some people over at another grill shared them with us," Senpai said. "Fresh too." They were good. Seasoned with just the right amount of sesame and salt. "It was a cute junior-high girl who gave them to me. I wanted to share some of our meat, but I couldn't find her again."

I glanced around. Didn't recognize anyone. I must have been overthinking it.

I swatted away a bug and took another big bite of red rice.

***

The sky cooled from orange to indigo. Buzzing insects and croaking frogs sounded the fall of night. The forest was alive. Ironic how loud it could get out in the wilderness.

From a paper tube Tsukinoki-senpai held at arm length, bright yellow streaks of light arced through the air, shifting green partway, then finally red before fizzling out. She flashed a toothy grin toward President Tamaki, who was too busy eyeing the rest of the fireworks to notice.

Senpai gave him a firm kick. "Those ones aren't lit, doofus."

"Huh? Hey, I'm just trying to decide which we should do next."

"O-okay, fine, what about this one? This one's big! It'll need both of us, so let's do this one!"

"Eh, you can handle it." *Smack.* "Ow, okay, fine, stop kicking me!"

The wedding bells in the distance were starting to get a little annoying.

I sighed and put one of the last remaining meat slices on the grill. The coals were still hot enough to get it nice and slow-cooked, which so help me God I would succeed at this time. I named her Setsuko.

Gunpowder popped somewhere. Yakishio had set off a pinwheel, sending Komari squealing for cover.

"Those two got friendly fast." Yanami nibbled on a bit of raw green pepper. Our definitions of friendly differed slightly.

"Not interested in the fireworks?" I asked.

"Gotta have dessert first."

"Oh, I think I catch your drift. Only one thing an open fire calls for."

Yanami chuckled. "You know it."

"Smore—"

"Offal!" Yanami produced a bag of mixed entrails. How silly of me. "This is always how we bookend our cookouts back home."

We had already edged too close to the Pandora's box that was Yanami's family situation before. I chose not to test fate again.

Setsuko was looking good. One side nice and brown. In human terms, I had just sent her off to elementary school. They grew up so fast. I went to flip her over and get the other side.

"Oh, dibs." Yanami snatched her up, and she was no more.

"Setsuko!" I cried. It happened so fast. There was nothing I could have done. Our memories together flashed before my eyes.

"Setsuwha?"

"Nothing."

Yanami snickered and held her chopsticks out. "All you had to do was ask. Here. Say 'ahhh.'"

"Wha? Huh?!" I looked left and right. No one was looking. I opened up and let her guide the fatty meat into my mouth.

"Good?" she asked.

"G-good."

"So how much?"

I nearly swallowed wrong. So that was how she was gonna play it. I felt cheated, but since she'd asked...

"S-seven—"

"I was just kidding, dude," she laughed. "Wait, what were you about to say? 700?"

I turned away. "N-no."

Yanami sneered. "I'm that in demand, huh? Good to know."

"L-look, most girls don't go around feeding every guy they see. It's a supply-side thing. That's all."

"Uh-huh, sure. Want another? I've got a sale going on."

I knew she was messing with me, and that there was no way to win—save for not to play. So I didn't.

Yakishio was off twirling by herself, fireworks in each hand. Sparks twinkled all around her before shimmering away into the dark ground. It was almost cute, the way she giggled and cheered to herself. She usually was, outside of actual conversation.

Komari, meanwhile, busied herself singing the ground with her own fireworks. I could only assume it had killed her family or something.

They with their fireworks and Yanami with her food, everyone was off having fun doing their own things. Now that Setsuko was no more and Yanami was busy with her "dessert," it was time to decide my own fate. I settled on fireworks. I made my way to the pile and found a small, gun-shaped one around the middle. It was a cheap thing, but I vividly remembered it being my favorite as a kid. I'd pretend to shoot at things, mostly just singe rocks on the ground. Kinda like Komari. I peeked at her while I lit the fuse.

She was kneeling down, trying to light a large tube firework on the ground to little success. After a few tries, the flame finally took, and the sparks flew—for a moment, at least, before stopping entirely. The gunpowder must have been damp. I lost interest.

And then she tilted the tube and peered straight down it.

"Don't—"

I could barely get a word out before it happened. There was a bang. A flash of light. Everything went white.

When my vision returned, the president was there next to her, the mouth of the tube crushed in his fist. He hurled the firework away.

"Komari-chan, are you hurt?!" he shouted.

"I-I'm—"

"Did it get you anywhere? Show me!" He inspected her hands, then grabbed her by the cheeks and turned her head this way and that. "Can you see? Do you feel any pain? Any at all?"

"N-no... I-I'm okay," Komari stammered.

"Oh, thank god." The president finally stopped scowling. "Don't ever do that again. You could have burned your face real bad."

"Th-there isn't much to...mess up anyway. Y-your hand—"

"I don't wanna hear it." He slipped the hand he'd stopped the firework with into his pocket. "Don't ever talk like that."

"N-no one wants to look at...*my* face. No one would see."

"You would."

"W-well, I..."

"*You* would look in the mirror every day, and every day you'd think back on today and regret it. I don't want that for you."

Komari opened and closed her mouth wordlessly. "Don't ever talk like that. I want you to care about yourself."

"P-President!" Komari finally cried out, her voice cracking. She breathed in deep, so deep I could hear it from where I stood, and then she said, "I-I love you!"

Time stopped. Yanami flipped some meat. Yakishio singed the back of her hair on a fountain firework.

The president didn't move. "Komari-chan, I don't..."

Another deep breath. "I...I have feelings for you! I always have! For the longest time! I lo... I'm in love with you!" She just kept talking like she couldn't hold it all back anymore. "I-I didn't think you really...paid much attention to me. But what you said. Just now. I-it means a lot to me." She started to trail off, each word eating twice the momentum of the last. "So, um, I l-love you! I want us to be t-together!"

When there was nothing more to be said, Komari simply hung her head low, tears at the verge of falling. Tsukinoki-senpai watched it all as still as a statue. Yanami ate her meat. Yakishio flailed at the cinders burning her back.

What an absolute circus troupe.

There was silence for a long time before the president finally said, "Sorry. You just, uh, surprised me a little." He opened his mouth to continue several times, only to close it again. He chose his next words carefully. "Can you give me some time to think?"

Time flowed again. Komari nodded. She met eyes with Tsukinoki-senpai, flinched, and sprinted away. I had a feeling I knew what was going on here.

The peanut gallery—Yanami, Yakishio, and I—exchanged glances.

Tsukinoki-senpai slowly approached the president. "What was that?"

"What was what?" he shot back. "It came out of nowhere, Koto. What was I supposed to say?" Tsukinoki-senpai yanked his hand out of his pocket and doused it in water. "Thanks. It's just soot. It's not burned that bad."

"Why would you lead her on like that? It's cruel. It's just cruel, Shintarou." She wrapped his hand in a handkerchief.

"Koto, I—"

"You know turning her down is the right thing to do!" Senpai gripped his hand hard and glared up at him with cold, lethal eyes.

"Koto, what are you talking about?"

"So why?!" she screamed. "Why didn't you?!"

The president couldn't hold her gaze. "Why does it matter to you? It's not your decision to make."

It got quiet again. Popping from the offal on the grill punctuated the droning insects.

"Right," Senpai said softly. "That's fair. We're only friends, after all." More silence—this time interrupted by a sharp slap against the president's cheek. "So sorry for getting it twisted!"

She was gone. President Tamaki stood alone. And a black snake firework squirmed between Yakishio's legs. How I yearned for that girl's blissful ignorance.

She and Yanami shot me urging glances. I considered finding one of those snakes for myself. They mouthed the word "go." There would be no peace.

"Uh, hey, Prez," I said.

He looked up but not quite at me. "Oh. Hey, Nukumizu. Sorry I went and screwed the trip."

"D-don't worry about it. We'll take care of things here. You should, uh, get going."

"Where? To whom?"

I had to physically stop myself from using harsh language. "I can't decide that for you." Not that I was making much of an effort to be polite.

"Right. Sorry. And thanks."

He stumbled off into the darkness. The rest of us heaved a much needed sigh of relief. Things had taken a hard and unexpected turn into the *real*.

"Um, excuse me." A camp employee awkwardly shuffled up to us. "We're about to start putting out grills if you guys don't mind cleaning up." Lord only knew how long they'd been waiting for a chance to speak up. I related heavily.

"Yeah, sorry. We'll get right on that," I said.

"So sorry to interrupt."

There was no reason they had to be that nice about it. I started throwing plates together.

"No problem." Yanami put on her toughest face. "I'll have this food gone in a flash."

***

"Man, who woulda thunk she had it in her. You go, Komari-chan." Yakishio squeezed her sudsy sponge and shared her passion with the twinkling night sky. "A confession under the stars with the guy who just put himself on the line to protect you. Gah, it's so dreamy! We're living in the best timeline, girls. It's our turn to be aggressive and take the bull by the..."—she dropped her sponge—"horns. Right. Guess I should take my own advice, huh?"

I tied my garbage bag shut. What was it about these loser heroines and pouring salt onto their own wounds?

"Hey, Nukkun," she said, "so Tsukinoki-senpai and the president *aren't* dating?"

"Doesn't seem like it," I replied. "I always figured they would be soon if they weren't already."

The president made it seem like Komari actually had a chance, though. Tsukinoki-senpai was the last person I'd expected to be up for potential loser status.

"Yah." Yanami nodded confidently as she stuffed her face with more offal. "Airuh hoo'd huffgl."

"Yeah, they *are* cute," Yakishio agreed.

"Aho deyhodly hadizhive honon hoo."

"Oh, totally, I felt it too."

Today I learned that Yakishio was bilingual. Something told me my input wouldn't be needed in this discussion, so I took my cue to bow out, using one of my famous Irish goodbyes. Those were my specialty. They wouldn't even know I'd left.

Eventually, I wandered over to the bathrooms, drawn to a single dim overhead light. It was as good a time as any to do my business.

The urinals there were totally open to the breeze at about eye level, allowing for a somewhat disturbing view of the trees and bushes whispering in the distance. The lack of company was similarly unnerving, though admittedly not as unnerving as the alternative.

"Nukumizu."

I yelped. Were they not already down, I would have needed another pair of pants. "P-Prez? Jesus, you scared the crap out of me!"

"I gotta talk to you, man."

"Cool, awesome, can I finish first?! And get your hand off my shoulder!"

I zipped up, thoroughly washed my hands, and recentered myself.

"So have you been here this whole time?" I asked.

"I... Well, I just don't know what to do."

You could start by doing what I said and going after one of them instead of crying to me about it mid-piss.

"I think I could use an ear right now," he said.

So he was looking for love advice. From me, of all people. And about a love *triangle*, no less. He genuinely would have been better off asking a worm how to outfly a bird. I gave him a look. "Um, so, I'll level with you. I really don't know what help I could realistically offer. You're kind of in a league of your own, dude."

"Okay, but look, I can count on one hand the number of relationships I've been in. It's zero. I've never been asked out, and the only Valentine's chocolate I ever get is from Koto."

"Ah, but you *do* get chocolate," I pointed out.

"And every time it's got 'friend' written on it. Every year, ever since we were kids. Where does she even find that?" Why were we talking about this around a bunch of urinals? What was this actual NPC interaction? "No one ever invites me when they go hang out with girls either. I'm seriously as loveless as it gets, man."

Little did he know of the true depths of lovelessness. Of how much worse it could truly be.

"Sure, but the fact that you're hesitating this much should tell you something," I said. "Maybe you actually do feel something for Komari."

"She's plenty cute, but I just never considered her...like *that*, you know?"

"Then why did you tell her you'd think about it?"

"Look, a girl like her confesses to a dork like me? You'd reconsider a few assumptions yourself."

Would I? Regardless, there was still one massive elephant in the room.

"What about Tsukinoki-senpai?" I asked. *She* was probably the biggest reason he'd never gotten chocolates or been asked out.

The president sagged his shoulders. "I guess there's no reason to be shy about it now."

"About what?"

"I've already asked her out," he said. "And she shot me down."

"Wait, what?" How was that possible? If those two weren't a thing, what hope was there for any of us? "You're not talking like when you were four or five, right?"

"What? No. It was last Christmas."

Not even a year ago. Suddenly, everything made sense. The president had been well on the rejection recovery path when in came an adorable little underclassman. She confessed, and now he was conflicted. No wonder. I couldn't blame him, even if it *was* a gremlin he was agonizing over.

"That's why I haven't been going to the club as much lately," he went on. "Koto just acts like nothing's changed." He got down on his haunches and hugged his knees. I almost reminded him people peed here. "But then you saw the way she snapped back there. I feel like I'm going insane, man. What was *that* all about?"

That was the question now. It didn't make sense for Tsukinoki-senpai to have blown up if she'd already made her position clear.

"Either way, nothing's gonna change the fact that you two need to talk." I put a hand on his shoulder. "I have a feeling there hasn't been enough of that."

"You sound like you know what you're talking about. Are you, like, an expert or something?"

I smiled sarcastically. "Yeah, just call me Casanova."

***

I returned to Yanami and Yakishio with instructions from the president to head back to the lodge. The rest was up to him. My role had ended utterly and entirely. I rolled my sleeves up to start helping with dishes.

"Nukumizu!" Yanami snapped. "Where have you been?!"

Someone was not happy. Maybe ditching while everyone was still cleaning had been a bad idea.

"I, uh, had to use the bathroom," I said.

"Yeah, great, who asked?" I was too shook to answer that question. "Listen. Tsukinoki-senpai just left with all her things!"

Huh. This late? Not very smart. I stared down at the direction she pointed.

A beat later, I realized she was staring back.

"Uh, hello?" Yanami fussed at me.

"Hm? Yeah?"

"You're just gonna let a girl go out at night all by herself?"

What did she want me to do—go after her? This late? Didn't sound very smart.

Yanami reeled back and smacked me in the shoulder. Hard. "Lemon-chan went after Komari-chan. I'm looking for the president. Get going!" she barked.

"Come on, it's pitch-black out—" She made a face that instilled in me far more fear of her than of the dark. "Yes, ma'am. On it."

I set off after Tsukinoki-senpai, lighting my way with my phone's flashlight. It didn't take long for me to stumble across a bus stop. In the dim light, I spotted a girl and her luggage. I called out to her.

"Oh. Nukumizu-kun." Senpai didn't try to hide her disappointment upon recognizing me. I, unfortunately, was not the president.

"Senpai, where are you going?" I asked. "The lodge is the other way."

"I'm going home. I just can't be around *him* right now." She readjusted the bag on her shoulder and resumed walking.

"Hey, hold on. The buses aren't running anymore, Senpai."

"I can make it to the station on foot."

That simply wasn't reasonable, not in this darkness.

"Can you please just sit so we can talk for a second?" I pleaded. "Whaddya know, there's a bench right here."

"Nukumizu-kun!" I had just yoinked her bag. "I don't have time for this."

"You can take a little break," I said. I sat down at the bus stop and offered a couple of drinks I'd bought beforehand. "Gogo or Kochakaden tea?"

Senpai sighed. "Gogo." She took a seat next to me. Mission accomplished.

I didn't actually know what to do next. I hadn't asked Yanami what exactly I was meant to say to her. I looked down the old wooded road.

"Did Shintarou send you?" she asked.

"Huh? Uh..."

Senpai frowned at me. "He didn't?"

"H-he did," I lied. "He went looking for you at the lodge, but I guess you just missed each other."

Please, Prez, don't you make me look stupid.

Tsukinoki-senpai took a sip of her tea, then slouched. "I'm really sorry this had to happen today."

Where had I heard that apology before?

I twisted the cap off my tea. This story would have had a quick and easy resolution were it only between her and Prez. Komari was the complicating factor here. Trigonometry was never my strong suit.

"How's Komari-chan?"

"I don't actually know," I replied. "Yakishio's looking for her. I wouldn't be too worried."

There was an awkward silence before Tsukinoki-senpai quietly spoke up again. "Men do like the quiet ones, don't they? The ones that make you feel like they need you."

Here came the heavy stuff. These people had to be beyond desperate if they were coming to *me* for advice.

"That is the stereotype, I suppose," I said.

"Like Komari-chan. I guess she kind of *is* the ideal."

Bold statement.

"I don't think what most men like is really relevant here. What's important is how you feel about each other, and, well, for what it's worth, I definitely got the vibe that the president was more interested in you than her."

"I know. I thought so too."

What was *that* about? Wasn't she the one who turned Prez down? Something wasn't adding up.

"You two need to talk," I said. "I think maybe that might make things more clear."

"What else is there to clarify? You heard what he said. He's 'thinking about it.' He doesn't know *who* he's interested in."

I stumbled over my words a few times, trying to decide how much I was allowed to say. "So, uh, here's the thing. The president… He, er, may kinda think you aren't into him."

"What?! Literally why?!"

I'd totally called it. The president hadn't been shot down. There was a massive misunderstanding at play here. I couldn't play my hand all at once at risk of screwing something up, so I decided to stay tactful.

"You two went out last Christmas, right? That information's accurate?" I asked.

"What did he tell you about that for?"

"Uh, humor me. So did he ever, I dunno, tell you anything that day?"

"Yes? He told me lots of things. We talk all the time."

"No, I mean, like, anything *important*. You know, about him, his feelings, that sort of thing."

"He did go on a rant about Dom Dom's burgers when we were at Mos Burger."

What kind of Christmas date night involved fast food? I had enough faith in the president to assume that hadn't been where the alleged confession happened.

"Where'd you go other than that?" I pressed. "Maybe a light show, somewhere with a scenic view. Was there any romance in the air at all?"

"With him?" She scoffed. "Not likely."

"Okay, maybe it wasn't a place, but did he ever do anything that stood out? Held your hands when they were cold? Share a scarf? Give you a cake with a ring inside? Did you gaze into each other's eyes the moment a bunch of lights flickered on while an Oda Kazusama love song played in the background?"

"Does anyone even remember who that guy is?"

I was grasping at straws. Where was that damn confession? Was Tsukinoki-senpai just dense enough that not even the Christmas spirit had been enough to get through to her?

"Come to think of it," she said, "there was one thing on our way home. He said something to me at the tree in front of the station."

Oh, thank god he moved past the Dom Dom thing. My faith in Prez had been restored.

"So what did he say?!"

"Well, he roasted me for a bit, and then he backtracked and was like 'don't worry' because he'd 'take me if no one wanted me.'"

Oh. Oh, that was worse than Dom Dom.

"What'd you tell him?" I asked.

"I told him to get out of my face and take a long walk off a short cliff." Senpai gave me a confused look. "What's this about, anyway?"

"Yeah. No. I don't even blame you. There's no reduced sentence coming with *that* confession."

What an absolute dumpster fire of a man. I started mentally collating rom-coms to recommend him for rehabilitation purposes.

"Conf... What?" Tsukinoki-senpai got real quiet. But not for long. "*What?!* That was a *what*?!" It was no longer quiet.

"I'm assuming he meant it in that indirect 'I wanna see you when I wake up every morning' sort of way."

Mystery solved. All that was left was to debate whether I should have said anything at all.

"And on *Christmas*?! Christmas. Second year of high school, and *that* was my Christmas confession?! What kind of... Is he mentally fucking deficient?!"

Answer: No. I should not have said any of that. The situation was hanging by a thread, and now it was my responsibility to fix it.

"I mean, I could be wrong. That's just my interpretation, so take it with a grain of—"

"I'm gonna straight up ban that son of a bitch!" Senpai shouted.

"Can we simmer down, please?"

Feet crashed against dirt and gravel. I turned around to find the president, shoulders heaving and out of breath. He stopped for a moment, then came closer.

"Prez!" I called out.

I was saved. The rest was up to them and no longer any of my business. I quietly and tactfully started to make my way back to the lodge, freed from the burden of a guilty conscience.

Out of nowhere, a hand emerged, sealed my mouth shut, and yanked me behind the tree line.

I tried to yell.

"Hush! They'll hear you!" It was Yanami. I nodded. Mostly for lack of another option. "Head down. This is for the good of the club."

Her whispers tickled my ear.

"Are you sure we should be—" She pinched my side. Message received.

I shrunk down below the shrubs and pricked up my ears. Our arms brushed as we shuffled into position. She smelled like smoke and sweat and Febreze.

Tsukinoki-senpai had her head down, her expression hidden. The president played with his hair nervously.

"I-I guess I should apologize," he said.

Senpai shot back, "I heard a lot from Nukumizu-kun. Is it true?"

"Did you talk about Christmas?"

She didn't answer. "We've been together for over a decade."

"Ever since we were old enough to be in school. Somehow always got the same class."

"I've never been the most feminine. Do you remember when those girls used to bully me?" She closed her eyes and bit her lip.

"We don't have to cross old bridges if it hurts, Koto."

"You stood up for me. You stood up for me, and you didn't care what they said about you."

"I can handle a few jerks," Prez said. He meant it. "Better me than you."

"See? That right there's what drove me insane." Even from far back, I could see the red creeping up her face. She held her hand up to her mouth. "You shot up in junior high. It wasn't easy keeping you to myself, you know."

"You make it sound like it was your fault I never peaked."

It was, I silently quipped.

"You're awful, you know that? I waited. And waited. And waited. And waited. And waited." She swallowed. Breathed. Swallowed again. Marched up to Prez. "And *that* was your confession?! You're unbelievable. Un*believable*! We could be soulmates from a past life and I'd *still* kick you to the curb!" She only stopped because she'd run out of air to shout with.

Prez laughed awkwardly. "Yeah. You're right." He made a clumsy smile and felt Tsukinoki-senpai's hair. She jumped. "But that's why I'm gonna make up for it in this one."

She bumped her head against his chest. "You can try."

After a moment's hesitation, the president wrapped his arms around her, and there he held her. More tenderly than glass.

***

"Whoa." Yanami's eyes were glued to them, hands pressed together.

We were overstaying our welcome for sure.

"We're leaving," I said.

"Dude, it's just getting good!"

"It's an invasion of privacy! We need to dip." I grabbed her hand and got moving. Truthfully, we needed to dip a long time ago.

"Nukumizu-kun."

"They need time alone," I said.

"And you need to keep holding my hand because...?"

I recoiled and yanked mine away at once. It was the mood. We'd been crouched together with all that romantic tension going around. It was making me loopy.

"S-sorry!" I stammered. "I-I didn't mean to!"

"You don't gotta apologize." She noticed me blushing and immediately flipped into bully mode. "Hey, do I get one? You gonna confess to me next?"

"No."

"Aww, c'mon. I promise I'll let you down easy."

"Not happening." I walked faster.

Yanami kept pace, still with that same smirk on her lips. "Don't you have a heart? Weren't you *moved* by that just now? Don't you want what they have?" She leaned over and fixed me in her annoyingly prying gaze.

"Sure, but not with someone who just said they were gonna turn me down."

"True. I will do that." No hesitation. "But play your cards right and maybe you can swipe yourself a smooch on the cheek at least."

"But you'll still reject me."

"Man, you're fussy." She shrugged. "Whatever. We got more important things to worry about."

"'Whatever'?"

She raised her eyebrows at me. "Did you forget Komari-chan? We gotta get back to the lodge and check on her."

"Right. Yeah. You're right." I cocked my head and lowered my voice. "'Whatever'?"

***

Locked. I had completely forgotten the door to the boys' room was locked. And the president had the key. One option was to wait in the girls' room for him to get back, but yeah, that wasn't happening. I still hadn't recovered from Yanami's brusqueness. She'd been all teasy and jokey, and then all of a sudden colder than the arctic. I didn't get women.

I hauled my tired legs out of the lodge. Maybe I'd find a stag beetle to empathize with.

I passed under a window and heard the latter end of a conversation. There was another group here besides us. Some student council trip for a bunch of local schools. I put some distance between myself and the commotion inside.

That was when I saw her, crouched in the shadows, orange cinders sputtering at the bottom end of a short, thin stick in her hand. It was Komari. Yakishio wasn't with her.

I made it to her before I could decide what to say. "Hey. There you are."

"Oh. Nukumizu. Wh-what do you want?"

It occurred to me too late the situation I'd put myself in. I recalled the image of Prez and Senpai in each other's arms, and I didn't have the courage to share it with her. It wasn't my place to, anyway. It had to come from the president himself.

Komari thrust a bag out at me. "Sp-sparklers. Too many for me to finish."

I crouched down, picked one, and set it alight. The cinders sputtered with unfamiliar vigor before retreating into a smoldering bud. A second of peace. The sparks returned, and this time I recognized the way they danced and popped.

"Hm. Different." I couldn't remember the last time I'd played with sparklers. Kaju and I were overdue.

We burned through stick after stick before I eventually found enough nerve to peek at Komari, and when I did, I found her peeking back.

"Wh-what?"

"Wasn't Yakishio with you?"

"Sh-she was. She did one. Then got bored and left."

You couldn't set much on fire with sparklers. Not her speed, I assumed.

"You guys seem like you really bonded," I said. "That's good."

Komari did not look like she agreed. "Y-you need to see an optometrist."

Is that an oxymoron?

We were getting somewhere, talking normally. She must have

been riding the adrenaline from the confession still. Just had to get her back to the room before tragedy could strike. The girls would be more equipped for it than me.

"Th-the president came. Before you did," she said.

My sparkler died after a pitiful few seconds of life. The bud at the end fell.

"Oh. And what did he...?"

"It's over." She handed me the bag and lit my new sparkler. "He turned me down."

She sounded numb.

"Oh... So he told you flat out, huh?"

Personally, I would have sat on it so I could have backup in case my first pick fell through.

"B-bet you'd have kept me as backup."

"How'd you know that?"

"B-because you're the worst."

Couldn't argue with that.

The buds on our fireworks smoldered for a while, then burst into sparks at nearly the exact same time, revealing the expression on Komari's face.

"But he... H-he thought about it. He really, actually considered it." She was smiling. It looked like it hurt. "I got one over on Tsukinoki-senpai... Even if only for a little while."

She shook. Her tiny shoulders trembled. The end of her sparkler fizzled out, and she watched as it fell to the ground.

"I-I'm gonna cry now," she choked. "So g-go away." She clung to that dead firework, the wind very nearly carrying her voice away. "Please."

I went back inside the lodge and found a bench to sit on and cracked open my canned coffee before realizing I didn't feel like drinking it. I didn't know how to feel.

The lobby's fluorescent lights buzzed and flickered overhead.

I thought about them. The five strangers who I'd come here with. What would we be once this retreat from reality was over? Yanami and Yakishio weren't *really* interested in the literature club. It was just a rest stop for them before they inevitably spread their wings and moved on to something else. Would Komari even feel comfortable continuing to show up? Would our senpai? We were a week away from summer vacation. What would happen to my lunches with Yanami?

I took a sip of coffee. Suddenly felt like writing.

***

The next morning, we gathered in a meeting room at the lodge.

"Uploading now." The president tapped the enter key with dramatic flare. With that, chapter one of my story—*Halfway Down Love Street*—was out for all to read. "Ended up quite a bit different from what we talked about."

Until recently, I'd planned on writing a slow-life isekai. Even I was still half surprised I had ended up making it a rom-com set in the real world.

"Inspiration just kinda struck," I said. It wasn't much. You could read the whole thing in less than three minutes. "I'll slowly add to it over time, I think."

"Good plan," Prez said. "Oh, hey, you've already got a comment on yours, Yanami-san."

"Oooh, really?" Yanami stopped munching on her melon bread long enough to lean in and get a look. Her lips curled up and eyes narrowed, darting to me. "Foundja, Nukumizu-kun."

"Y-yeah. That's me," I admitted. Everything was all topsy-turvy. The *author* was supposed to get nervous about their readers, not the other way around.

"Hm. Thanks. By the way, what're those 'points'?"

"You get those anytime someone bookmarks or rates any of your work," the president said, sucking on some fruit juice. "You've got two comments, actually." He reached to take the mouse from Yanami.

"Th-that might be me." Komari entered with just her gym clothes thrown on. An uncomfortable breeze ran through the room, but she didn't seem to care. She came straight up to the president.

"Komari-chan," he said. "Morning."

"G-good morning. Did you g-get my story?" She bowed her head. "If you'll...help me upload it. Please."

Prez pulled the laptop back to him. "Sure. Yeah," he replied, nodding a few times. "There it is. And that's your title and blurb. All set." He started to fill in the upload form, then paused. "As is?"

"As is, please." Komari gulped. "I like my title. And I don't want to split it up. I want that to be chapter one."

There were no stops or stutters. She said what she meant to, and you could see it in her eyes. The president certainly did.

"Gotcha," he said. "I think you're right. People will appreciate it better this way." He smiled at her, then faced the computer again. "It's done. There it is."

Komari squinted at the screen, saw her work, and smiled. "Th-thank you. I don't really...get Narou. Could you maybe teach me about it sometime?"

"Absolutely."

I didn't recognize this Komari. The Komari I was familiar with usually had a scowl or scrunched nose. Maybe that was just me.

There was still one more loose end in the room. Tsukinoki-senpai sat at a different table, noticeably more quiet than usual.

Komari clenched her fists a few times before marching over and taking a seat across from her. "G-good morning, Senpai."

"Good... Good morning, Komari-chan," Senpai replied.

No one said anything for a few seconds. The silence was suffocating, until Komari finally broke it. "I-I want you to read my story."

"Okay. I'll be sure to comment."

"Th-thanks..." Another awkward moment of nothing. "P-please be at the club tomorrow. It would feel...empty without you." She hung her head. "Also, the student council lady is scary."

Tsukinoki-senpai beamed. "Y-you got it, Komari-chan! I'll be there! She won't touch you while I'm around!" With the same explosive force that her smile had returned, tears began streaking down her cheeks. "Huh? Crap, sorry, I...I don't mean to..."

Komari scurried next to her. "I-I'm okay, Senpai. Really."

"I just... I don't know what I was gonna do if you stopped coming." She sniffed. "Thank you, Komari-chan. Thank you."

Komari wrapped her arms around Senpai and held her for a long while.

Tsukinoki-senpai wiped her eyes, recomposing herself. "I always love reading your stories. I can't wait to see this one."

"Th-thank you. What about yours? Did you write anything?"

"Ah, well, the censors went a little crazy on mine. It's barely a full page now." She waved her phone around, still sniffling. "I'm offended someone would imply what I write is smut."

Is it not? The numbers sure seemed to imply otherwise.

"L-let's go sit with everyone else."

"Yeah. We should."

They came over hand-in-hand. The president had the biggest smile.

This was no happily-ever-after. Not for everyone. President Tamaki and Tsukinoki-senpai were together, but at the cost of rejecting Komari. That was just the truth of the matter. Things would have to change. Slowly but nonetheless surely, as relationships always did. Change was a fact of life. I'd simply managed to evade it for longer than most.

But it would catch up to me one day, if it hadn't already. Here I was, after all. Caught in a web of ever-evolving people. I got a strange sense of wonder, seeing it unfold so up close.

A (slightly darker than usual) tawny hand slid a piece of paper to me. "Here, Nukkun. Can you put this on that what's-it-called site for me?"

"What is this? You doing a picture journal?" I asked.

"Yup. I found some colored pencils in the lobby, so I figured why not."

It was a drawing of the beach. I noted a somewhat Yakishio-esque figure holding hands with another figure on the ground.

"Is that me?"

Yakishio snickered. "Sure is, detective. That's you right there."

Out of context, I could see someone thinking she was dragging a corpse across the beach.

"Hey, I like that," Prez interjected, peering over. "Can't put this on Narou, though. That's for text only."

"Why don't we make a club Twitter account and put it on there?" I proposed.

The president clapped. "That's perfect. We actually already have one, just don't use it for anything."

Tsukinoki-senpai sniffled again and took the picture. "I saw a scanner in the office, I think. I'll ask if we can borrow it. Come with me, Yakishio-chan."

Off they went together.

I pulled up my post on my phone, just to see it. Strange feeling, having something you worked on out in the open like that.

"Whoa, I've already got a comment and a rating."

Ever so trepidatiously, I took a look. The rating was the lowest possible and the comment read, "This guy's a virgin."

Well, that was just plain rude. Where was the block button again? But wait, how did they know I was a virgin?

"Komari," I growled. "I know this was you."

She curled her lips into a condescending smile. "K-keep posting, and maybe I'll adjust it."

"I will. You think I won't, but I will."

Too Many Losing Heroines!

INTERMISSION

She's Right Behind Me, Isn't She?

AMONG THE MANY FACES ADDING TO THE LOW DIN of the cafeteria, one in particular stood out like a sore thumb. She tied her bright brown hair into a loose ponytail and looked lazily up at the poster on the wall.

"Toyohashi Student Council Coalition Meet—Junior & High School Divisions."

Shikiya Yumeko, second-year secretary of Tsuwabuki High School's student council, stood at the ready to serve whoever came up in line, in the meantime keeping watch on her underclassman busily attending to their own duties.

One in particular caught her white-tinted eye. A young girl in an apron was working fast, faster than the line could move. She served a mound of rice with a ladle of curry to its side on one plate before the next was even ready. Shikiya even suspected she was taking gender into account—more for boys, slightly less for girls. She picked up a spare plate with a serving meant for one of the boys.

A smirk snuck up on her.

The amounts weren't different at all. It only *seemed* like the women's mounds of rice were smaller, and the girl was simply hiding the rest beneath the curry.

"Girls, your plates are over here!" she announced. "Salad's coming soon!"

"You," Shikiya said, softly as ever. "I like your ethic."

The girl jumped slightly. She turned to Shikiya, her eyes darting between the secretary's exposed shoulders and navel. "Naughty..."

"I'm...sorry?"

"Ah, my apologies. Just admiring how fashionable and mature my Tsuwabuki betters are."

"You wouldn't be the first," Shikiya breathed.

The girl handed a tray with salad to a student from another school and shouted more instructions. Things were moving like a well-oiled machine.

"Are you...interested in our school?" Shikiya asked.

"Yes, I am, as a matter of fact. My brother's a first-year there. I'm hoping we'll get to attend together in a couple of years." Her smile was bright and refined. She removed her hair wrap, long black strands spilling down her back. "Today has been an invaluable experience. Would you mind if I asked you more about your school later?"

"Not at all... Would you like to sit together?" Shikiya searched the sea of people until she found someone waving at her—Houkobaru Hibari, Tsuwabuki's student council president.

"I'd love to!" The girl scanned the sea herself as she folded up her apron. Everyone had a plate.

"Weren't you…? Earlier," Shikiya said, "weren't you cooking something? Red rice?"

"Oh, yes." She held a finger up. "Just to say hi."

"I…see." Shikiya didn't ask. "I'm a secretary at Tsuwabuki… Shikiya. Yumeko. You are?"

The girl picked up a (deceptively heavy) plate of curry and smiled. "Nukumizu Kaju, Momozono Junior High general affairs. Nice to meet you!"

Too Many Losing Heroines!

LOSS 4

When You Gaze upon the Losing Heroines, the Losing Heroines Gaze Back

MONDAY MORNING. I RESTED AN ELBOW ON MY desk, listening in and out of the myriad conversations going on in the classroom. Some were about shows on TV, some were about the baseball game, others about mutual friends, and still others about unfinished homework. Some were bold enough to humblebrag about how difficult their significant others could be.

Normal topics, all of them. Normal topics for normal people who lived normal lives together with other normal people. Normalcy came naturally to my classmates.

"Morning!"

Yakishio Lemon came bursting into the room. Several greeted her back. So much for my brooding.

She came straight up to my desk and thunked her bag on it. "Morning, Nukkun! The trip was fun, huh?"

"Er, uh, m-morning," I stammered out.

"Anyway, so here, this is yesterday's." She slipped a piece of paper out of her bag and handed it to me. Another entry for the picture journal already. This time it depicted a girl sprinting alongside a moving train.

"When did this happen?"

"Fell asleep on the way home last night. That's when I had to run back to my stop."

Interesting choice of tableau.

"We'll get it posted," I said.

"Thanks!"

She headed to her seat, waving at and high-fiving a few friends on the way. Where did she get that kind of energy this early in the morning?

Not all of us shared her enthusiasm. I stretched, my social batteries already running low, and let my eyes wander over to Yanami. She'd been spending less time with Hakamada Sousuke and his girl Himemiya Karen and more with a different group of friends. She was chatting with them now, as a matter of fact. That bubbly smile so rarely seemed to leave her face.

She noticed me staring and directed it at me. I pretended not to see. We never acknowledged each other in class. It wasn't intentional—we simply occupied a weird space between kind-of-secret and not at all.

Scattered laughter came from the classroom next door. Amanatsu-sensei must have waltzed into the wrong class again. It happened at least twice a month. Our class knew the drill and started making their way back to their seats.

Another normal day that we'd never see again.

***

Yanami left moments after lunch break started, but I waited a little bit before following. I considered it one of our unspoken rituals. I made a detour to grab some milk at the vending machine before heading to the usual spot.

Just as I was about to cut around to the back of the building, I heard a group of girls laugh. I stopped short of the corner. They were classmates, and I recognized the voices. Most probably would. They were a loud and gaudy bunch—my one weakness. I calculated a route to skirt around them in my head, and then I heard a name.

Yanami.

Their voices were low and callous. I stabbed the straw into my milk and sipped.

"Like how does it even happen, y'know? After all that work she put in, some transfer student pulls the rug out from under her."

"I'd literally stop coming to school."

Laughter. Yanami had mentioned things being uncomfortable, assumptions being made. Now I understood.

I doubted they'd say any of this to her face, but words could linger. People didn't necessarily have to say things out in the open for someone to hear what was being said.

This was what Yanami had been dealing with while I went around reviewing water fountains.

I started to leave. I wanted nothing to do with it.

"But did you hear? They're saying she's got her eye on someone else now."

That made me stop.

"She does?!" a couple others shouted.

She does?

If Yanami had a boyfriend, she hadn't hinted at it during the trip. For what I liked to think were obvious reasons, I glued myself to the wall, quieted my breathing, and listened even harder to the clique's shrill voices.

"Who is it? I know the basketball captain was talking to her the other day."

"It's that, uh... What's his name? Nuku... Nuku...mizu?"

"Nuk-who?"

There was someone else in this school named Nukumizu?

Wait, no there wasn't.

Are they talking about me?!

This was bad. Where had I gone wrong? Was I not careful enough? Had someone seen us eating together? At the family restaurant maybe? On the trip?

"I sorta kinda remember that guy? He's the one who's, like, right in the middle of the class roster."

Evidently, that was my most defining quality.

My thoughts continued to race at mach speed, and meanwhile the girls had gone quiet. One spoke up rather loudly. "Come on, Yanami's got it going on! She can do way better than him."

"For real. Bad taste, honestly."

"He's probably ugly."

What little I knew of Yanami rushed through my head. She was still in love with Hakamada. If this rumor spread...

"Honestly, she kinda got on my nerves. Like, get over yourself, y'know? Most halfway decent guys can probably see the red flags."

"Yeah, honestly, they probably deserve each other."

More laughter. I only stuck around long enough to hurl away my now-crushed milk box.

***

"What was *that* all about, Nukumizu-kun?" Yanami was ready and waiting at the fire escape.

"Wh-what was what?"

"Didn't you see me look at you? Why'd you ignore me?"

"Hey, I was trying to be subtle. You know, so everyone in class doesn't catch on to us hanging around each other."

The laughter echoed inside my head. Something I couldn't describe grabbed my heart and squeezed.

"Bit late for that," Yanami said. "We're in the same club, dude. We can *talk*, at least."

"Okay, okay, I'm sorry. I wasn't trying to ignore you."

"Better not have." She pulled out today's lunch. "That trip sure was eventful, huh?"

"Yeah. Yeah, it was." There were a lot of words to describe it, but I had to admit I'd also add "fun" to the list.

I'd written a little bit more of my story. Writing always seemed like a purely solitary affair to me. This project felt different, though I couldn't place why. Having people in it with you was new to me.

"I got to show off my cooking skills, so I'm happy," she said. "Now, I present today's lunch!"

The former half of that statement was questionable, but I could confirm the latter. Today's was sandwiches. Not convenience store sandwiches—actual handmade sandwiches. I saw ham and lettuce, egg, and a mysterious third variety with slices of a green something-or-other in it.

I picked the mystery one. "Cucumber. And is that Moromi miso?"

Morokyu: a tasty snack that combined the satisfying crunch of a cucumber with the salty sweetness of miso. And it was now in sandwich form.

"Go on and try it! I wanna know how it tastes."

I gave it a bite. "Mh, yeah. Surprisingly good. You might be onto something here." If you ignored the soggy cucumber bread. "I think some margarine would really elevate this."

"Ah, shoot, forgot that. How bad's that gonna hurt the price?"

I'd nearly forgotten about that. What was the tab even at again?

Good sandwiches took a surprising amount of work to put together. That in mind, I was leaning toward 500 yen at least.

Honestly, they probably deserve each other.

I heard the girls again.

Yanami was fun, pretty, and a class icon. I was a background character. We didn't deserve each other.

I was a parasite.

"Nukumizu-kun?"

"2,867 yen," I said.

"Whoa, no way, that's a new record! Wait." Yanami cocked her head. "Isn't that how much I owe you?"

"Guess it is. You're debt free."

"Okay, I'm flattered and all, but they're just sandwiches." She looked at them, perplexed, then at me.

Yanami Anna was an enigma I hadn't even begun to crack. I couldn't make heads or tails of her. When was she joking? When was she being serious? Roll the dice. Win or lose, she'd come out smiling.

"It's just starting to feel like I'm extorting you or something. I dunno. Just doesn't feel right."

Hers wasn't the type to involve themselves with guys like me. She belonged at the top. She was attractive. She was bubbly. She was popular. She was goofy. She was admittedly kind of a crybaby.

"Thanks for all the food," I said. "It was good."

She was a heroine, and she was a damn respectable one. Hakamada didn't know what he was missing.

Quietly, calmly, Yanami finally replied, "We started this because I needed to pay you back, sure, but I haven't hated it. It's been fun." She took a morokyu sandwich and bit into it. "Feels icky to end things like that."

I stared at the cross-section of bread, cucumber, and miso, and against my better judgment told her, "People are starting rumors about us."

I watched for her reaction. Found none. She eyed a bit of cucumber-stained bread.

"I'm sure you don't want people assuming things about you." I couldn't stop talking. The silence scared me. "You've got so many friends, and I don't think I'm the kind of guy you—"

"Slow down, please. I'm trying to understand." Yanami lidded the bento box. "Have I done something to upset you?"

"No, that's...!" I stopped, shook my head, and lowered my volume. "It's not that."

"You sure?"

I looked away. It wasn't her that made me upset.

The Yanami I had come to know, even if only a little, was in love with Hakamada. The Yanami I knew now, and who sat next to me, was in love with Hakamada.

What upset me was that people were ascribing things to her that weren't her. Feelings she didn't feel.

"I just don't like what people are saying."

I stared down at the half-eaten sandwich in my hand. Yanami said nothing, but I could feel her searching for the words.

She put the bento box on my lap. "Okay," she said. "Okay." She spoke firmly, her words cutting deep. "I'll stop talking to you then." She stood. "Thanks for the memories. Bye, I guess."

And that was it. She was gone. She left, bento box and all.

A few words. A few words were all it took to end it all. She hadn't even looked back. A part of me wished she had.

I opened the bento box. Meticulously crafted sandwiches were crammed together, end to end. In the corner, I noticed two cherry tomatoes for decoration. She would have woken up early to put all this together—this little ritual just for us.

It was then that I started to realize the magnitude of what I'd truly lost.

Three days to the closing ceremony.

***

I didn't eat much for dinner that night. Bed was too comfortable.

I went over the conversation in my head again for the umpteenth time, reconvincing myself that I'd done the right thing. We weren't together, not romantically or platonically. The relationship we had would have ended sooner or later.

Different worlds.

But more than that, I couldn't stand being the reason people had started to badmouth her.

"Oniisama, you seem down. Did something happen at school?"

Kaju suddenly materialized next to me in bed, ending the merry-go-round my thoughts had become.

"Little sisters aren't supposed to sneak into brothers' beds, Kaju." Even my quips lacked their usual energy. The ceiling was too interesting.

Kaju giggled and poked my cheek. "Did someone get rejected?"

"In a sense, I suppose."

That set her off. "I knew it! I knew you'd been acting strange lately!"

"Huh? Wait, no, not like that. Who would the girl even be?"

Yanami's ditzy smile came to mind. I turned over, facing my back to Kaju.

"Is it that girl I saw you grilling with? She was cuuute."

I shot up. "H-how do you know about her?!"

"That got your attention." Kaju grinned.

"Were you there? How much did you see?"

"Maaaybe I'll tell you. If you tell me about her." She mischievously put a finger up to her lips. "Or are you going to *make* me talk?"

I ignored the latter statement and flopped back down. "She's just a clubmate. And for the record, she's into someone else."

"It must be the short-haired girl then. I think an outgoing kind of person like her would be good for you."

"Another clubmate who's into someone else."

She thought for a moment, then clapped her hands together. "The mature one with the glasses? Though I'm curious about her role in whatever chaos I saw ensue."

"Dating the club president."

"There was another, but she didn't strike me as particularly remarkable." Kaju frowned. "No. You must keep an open mind, Kaju. Oniisama's judgment never errs."

I went ahead and assumed she had seen pretty much everything.

"Would you listen to me? I'm just tired from the trip. That's all." I rolled away from her again. "Your brother wants to sleep. Go to your room."

"I will not budge a single nanometer until you tell me which girl has stolen your heart. Plans have to be put in order, you know. I have to discern for myself whether they're really—"

She yiped as I threw the blanket over her and wrapped her up in it. That would buy me some peace.

"Ahhh, Oniisama's scent," Kaju sighed. This girl had some problems. "Yes, I can feel us becoming one. I see now. I will find a partner for you, dearest Oniisama. This I swear."

I threw the whole comforter on top of her next, for good measure. Back to my thoughts.

Everything replayed again. I went over it all—every choice,

every word she and I shared—and again I found no answer, nor its question.

Current tab: 0 yen.

***

Two days to the closing ceremony.

I was back to my solo lunch, though the fire escape remained an attractive spot to eat it. After finishing up some tuna bread and milk, I wrote a bit on my phone, then made for class again when it got closer to time.

It had only been a day, and yet our get-togethers already felt like a distant memory. Maybe that was all they were. I had to remind myself that they had been real.

I went straight to my seat, noting the clock for when the bell would chime. I watched Yanami chat with her friends out of the corner of my eye.

"Why do you look all down in the dumps, Nukkun?" Yakishio crouched down and planted her elbows on my desk, penciling herself into my alone time.

"That's just how I look," I said.

Unfortunately, I was still brooding and didn't have the patience to deal with her at that moment. Puppy dog eyes or no.

"That all it is?" she wondered aloud. "You seem awfully interested in a certain someone." I silently cursed her for saying that here, in the middle of the classroom of all places. A smile crept up her extra-tanned cheeks. "Hey, none of my business. If I were you, though, I'd say something. Before you regret it."

"Before I...?"

Yakishio smacked me on the back and turned her smile into a toothy grin. "Take it from someone who had to learn the hard way."

***

The hallway to the club room was deserted. It got me to thinking just how long the day had been. Where before I would have spent the former half of the day thinking about lunch, then the latter half remembering it, now the minutes seemed to trickle by. I could have counted them and all the nothingness that occupied the space between.

"What am I, a dog?" I muttered.

Lit club was my sole remaining obligation. Mostly Komari just griped and glared at me, but it was a convenient way to wait out the crowds after school.

I turned the knob. Unlocked. The first one here was always either me or Komari. I entered, ready for daggers, and got something else.

I froze.

"Yanami-san."

She pulled her hand back from a high-up shelf. Whatever she felt upon seeing me, her eyes didn't betray it. "Oh. Nukumizu-kun. Long time no see."

It hadn't been. We'd had lunch just yesterday. We were in the same class. I couldn't decide whether to point that out.

"You're still coming," I said. "For...how long?"

"I'm just returning some books I borrowed. Got plans with a friend later, so I was just leaving." She slung her bag over her shoulder. She didn't look at me again.

I felt it then. As she started to leave. Something inside was screaming at me. I couldn't describe it. It didn't make sense. But I knew.

This was my last chance.

"Yanami-san, can I say something?"

"What? My friend's waiting." She still didn't look at me. There was an edge to her voice that made me hesitate. "I can't stand here forever."

"Wait!" I thought of her and Yakishio. The weight of the regret they shared. The burden of missing your chance. "I think I... I actually, um, really enjoyed it. The lunches we had together." The strength with which Komari faced a losing battle. "I just..."

"You just?"

I just...what? We weren't a couple. We weren't even friends.

So what were we?

A lender and a debtor.

"I just...wanted you to know. It was fun."

Yanami gripped the doorknob and stood there for a while. And when that while was up, she simply said, "Okay."

The door opened. The light from the hallway poured in, obscuring whatever expression she wore when she finally turned around.

"I'm gonna go now," she said.

***

Nothing happened for the rest of that day. And then it was the next. The closing ceremony was tomorrow.

The classroom was more alive than usual, what with summer vacation right around the corner. Amanatsu-sensei almost handed out our report cards early, to no one's surprise. The people loved her for it.

The last lunch break of the semester came. I occupied my spot at the fire escape yet again, nibbling on curry bread and entertaining myself by staring at nothing. Afternoon practice for the sports clubs had been suspended on account of the heat, which didn't stop Yakishio, of course. Seeing a teacher practically drag her away from the track was about as much show as I got with my lunch.

"Girl's crazy."

I squinted at the breeze rushing across the field and shielded my bread from the dust cloud riding it. That was when I heard the footsteps clicking down the stairs behind me.

I sat up straight.

"O-oh. There you are." None other than Komari Chika in all her huffy glory came over and helped herself to the spot next to me.

"What're you doing here?" I asked.

"Y-you're literally the one who invited me." I cursed past me. "And I heard you got…rejected." A smug grin plastered itself across her face. "C-couldn't help coming to laugh at you."

Little bit short on sugar for the coating there.

"Where'd you even hear that?"

"You k-kinda shoved it in my face at the clubroom yesterday."

"You've got the wrong impression. Yanami and I aren't like that."

"S-sore loser." Komari dug around in a bag and pulled out a roll—the kind you could find by the half dozen at the store—that she promptly started munching on. "Wh-who gave you permission to go off and b-be happy?"

"Who's the sore loser again?"

"Sh-shut it!"

Everyone seemed keen on jumping to the same conclusion. Did we really look that into each other? What we had wasn't like that. It was...

What *did* we have?

I smiled mockingly at myself. Nothing. What we had was nothing. She owed me money, she paid me back. The transaction was done, and so were we.

Suddenly, I didn't feel like eating. I slid my bread back into its packaging.

"That all you're eating?" I asked. Komari bit into her second roll, still huffy from my last comment. She didn't even have anything to drink, I noticed. I offered my milk. "Here. Don't choke."

"Huh? B-but that's yours."

"I've got tea in a water bottle."

Komari eyed the milk box greedily. "No additives..." Then she snatched it and poked the straw right in.

Watching her suck it down made it feel like I was feeding a stray cat—which, come to think of it, you weren't supposed to do. You had to either ignore them or take them home. No in between.

Komari noticed me staring and pulled away. "N-no takesies-backsies."

As it happened, mine was a no-pets household.

***

Komari and I didn't talk much. I ended up leaving halfway into the break. She could have my oasis for the day.

"There you are! Nukumizu, I wanted to—hey! Hold up, dude!"

"Huh?" I stopped next to some guy, having nearly walked straight past him. It was him—Hakamada Sousuke. "Uh, can I help you?"

Busy day today.

"Mind coming with me?" he said. "Wanna go somewhere a little more private."

I followed him around the back of the old annex. It didn't take much to guess what sort of business he had with me.

"Sorry to bug you like this, man. I think you know what I wanted to—" I started to pull out my wallet. "Uh, why're you doing that?"

"Oh. Sorry. Just assumed." I shoved it back in my pocket. Wrong guess.

"Didn't take you for a jokester," Hakamada laughed. He could take me for whatever he wanted if it meant skimming over that miscommunication. He stammered a bit. "So, look, you've been hanging around Anna a lot, yeah?"

I had to take a second to attach the name to Yanami. "Huh?! W-well, I, er... I dunno. Not really."

Hakamada relaxed a little. "Hey, you can be real with me. You're that couple people have been talking about, aren't you? The one that hangs around the old annex. I heard something about a proposal, someone said you were getting all cuddly one time—everyone knows about it."

How had so much been so perfectly taken out of context? This was just silly.

"You've got it all wrong," I said. "Okay, well, not *all* wrong, but it's not like that!"

"You don't gotta be shy about it. These things just happen."

These things did *not* just happen, and I wished they'd *stop* happening. What did he want from me anyway? Was he about to shake me down and tell me to back off his best friend? Hakamada was pretty sporty. I didn't have a shot in hell against him one-on-one, but hey, I was a man. I could last a cool two seconds if push came to shove.

Hakamada shot his head down. "Take care of her for me!"

Take what of who now?

"Wait, wait, wait, you're seriously not understanding something!"

"I'm happy for you guys. I really am. I just want the best for Anna, and it means a lot to meet the guy her heart's set on."

"Look, you need to listen."

What was this guy's problem? Was he deaf or just one of *those* protagonists?

"Sorry to spring this on you," he went on. "I know we never really talked. Just thought we might change that."

"Okay, great, but you're not listening."

The guy had already friend-zoned Yanami. Logically, there was nothing to be gained, no reason this should have gotten me heated.

But it was.

He flashed one of his perfect, innocent smiles. "The four of us should go on a double date someti—"

"Can you stop for a second?"

"Oh, my bad. I'm rambling, aren't I?"

I didn't care that he was rambling. I didn't care for his apologies.

What I cared about was one thing and one thing only.

Something compelled me to step right up to him. "You know that she loved you, right?"

"I... Hey, did I say something?"

"You do, don't you?"

She wasn't my friend. I had no business saying these things. So why was I?

Hakamada recoiled, flitted his eyes around, and scratched at his nose nervously. "I mean, I had a feeling. That's why I was glad to hear she found someone else."

"Well, she still does!" I shouted. "She *still* loves you! Present tense! And it's not right for you to just pretend that she doesn't because of some stupid rumor!" It occurred to me a little late that I wasn't sure where I was going with this. Right. There was one more thing. "It's not true, by the way."

"Then why were you two having lunch together all the time?"

I had to stop myself from telling him that it was because he'd saddled Yanami with the bill after having a steak so he could go pick someone else. Not that Yanami was any less guilty with her udon dessert.

"Maybe you guys just eat too much," I said.

"What?"

We were getting further from the point with every word.

"Talking to myself."

This guy could not be real. It was like every rom-com protag had been stuffed in a blender and mixed into one.

In the midst of my self-aggrandizing, Hakamada suddenly froze solid like he'd seen a bear. Which was ridiculous, because there were no bears this far away from—

I followed his gaze, and behind me was something worse than a bear.

"Anna!" Hakamada yelped.

"Hey, guys," she said. She was shaking like a volcano about to erupt. "So, um, quick question. What's going on here?" Her face was bright red, and I couldn't tell if it was from rage or embarrassment.

"Yanami-san! Wh-what are you doing here?" I stammered.

"Komari-chan messaged me and said you were getting mugged by some hot guy. That it would make 'very good material.' So I came, just to be safe." She mad-dogged Hakamada, then me. "Now will someone please answer my question?"

That would be difficult, because not even I was sure what we were doing anymore. Or what Komari's ominous "material" was, for that matter.

"Lemme make this easier," Yanami said. "Nukumizu-kun. What were you just telling Sousuke?"

"That, uh, the limited edition Garigari-kun mint chocolate popsicle is actually the bomb?"

"I'm going to give you one more chance before I totally lose it."

We had already crossed that line. I could see it in her eyes.

Regardless of how screwed we already were, I had only one option: deny, deny, deny. Because for some reason that tended to work out better than confessing. The wonders of the justice system.

"Hold on!" Hakamada blurted. "It's not his fault. I'm the one who forced him to spill everything. I wouldn't listen."

I would have been moved by his selfless attempt to defend me if it hadn't simultaneously condemned us.

Yanami shook even harder. "Everything?! How much is *everything*?!"

Her tremors were exceeding chihuahua levels and nearing the Richter scale. Hakamada grabbed her shoulders in (what I could only assume was) an attempt to calm them. "I'm sorry, Anna. I just wanted you to find someone new."

"What?" The color left Yanami's face, the context finally dawning on her. "No. Don't start that," she whispered. Her bite was gone. She was so small now.

"I just want you to be happy," Hakamada continued, entirely oblivious. "To find someone who can treat you better than a guy like me ever could."

"Stop it." She looked moments from crumbling.

My body moved on its own. I threw Hakamada off and stood between them. "She said stop it, man!"

It was stupid. I was a million kinds of out of line. And I didn't care.

"Listen, and really listen this time, Hakamada! You're free to date or not date whoever you want. Reject Yanami-san, reject the whole damn world, I don't give a rat's ass!" I could feel Yanami staring daggers at me for real this time. I was so dead. "But you're not free to decide how she feels! Okay?! What happens to the things she *actually* feels then?! The things she feels for *you*?!"

The hot air that had been sweltering inside me for days was all coming out at once.

"You're the *one* person she doesn't want to hear that crap from! You can't tell her to be happy! You can't tell her to move on! You lost that right when you broke her heart!"

Hakamada. Man, that guy. What an ass. The way he stood there all cool and suave while I blustered like an idiot. He had it all. The looks. The personality. He didn't need to put on airs. He really was just that decent a guy.

Yanami and I were nothing in comparison. We weren't special or close like they were.

But I had seen strength and sadness he hadn't.

"You're supposed to be her friend! *You* rejected her! So own it! Quit using her to make yourself feel better about your own stupid guilty conscience!"

I started to hack and cough. Shouting didn't come naturally to me.

Hakamada hurriedly patted me on the back. "Hey, you all right?"

"F-fine..."

What a sorry display. If I had half of what Hakamada had, maybe I wouldn't lose my temper and then totally flub the landing. Maybe I would have had the courage to say the things I should have said to Yanami when it mattered most.

My head cooled, lethargy came hard and fast.

"You're right," Hakamada said. "You're absolutely right, Nukumizu."

"O-oh. Um. Sorry for going off like that."

He offered a hand. Timidly, I offered my own. And then we—

"Will you people stop screaming about my relationship status?!" Yanami roared, shoving her way between us. "What the hell is wrong with you two?! Who said you could go tying all my business up in a pretty little bow?! Uh, hello! I'm here too! Do you have tapioca for brains?!"

"I-I, uh..." I had nothing to say.

Yanami had her foot on the gas, and she was straight flooring it. First in line for vehicular manslaughter was Hakamada.

She grabbed him by the shirt and pulled him close. "Yes, I love you! I always have, and I still do! I am not over it—not even a little!"

"Anna, I—"

"Don't you dare apologize!" Yanami's eyes raged with over a decade of unspoken feelings. She buried her face in his chest. "I'm not over you, and you're just going to have to deal with that!"

"I love you! And I'm going to keep loving you! So shut up and go be happy with her! Go be happy with Himemiya Karen and let me deal with it!"

Yanami stayed there for a while, quietly shaking. Meanwhile, I was getting the feeling I was overstaying my welcome.

Before I could find the right timing to dip, she pulled away from him. "I'm going to keep loving you, and you're gonna have to deal. One day I'll stop loving you, and you'll have to deal with that too!" She let go of his shirt, shoving him away.

She then set her sights on me next. I shuddered.

"Nukumizu!" she barked. "What was I going to say to you?!"

"Um, I'm not sure," I said.

"Me neither! Totally forgot! It was probably nothing!"

She whacked me on the head.

"Ow! What was that for?"

"No reason!"

Well then, that was just mean.

Yanami pressed her finger against my chest and got in my face. "Now, I know you were trying to be sweet, but you can't go jumping to conclusions about who loves who, and I think this, and she thinks that, and then running your mouth! You're supposed to talk about these things first! *Communicate!*"

"But I...thought I couldn't."

She rolled her eyes hard. "Says who? Use your words! It's not against the rules!"

"It's not?"

"Dude, whose permission do you think you need to talk to someone at school? On what planet do you live?!"

None of this computed with my brain. On my home planet, chatting up girls was the ultimate faux pas.

"I dunno, I just thought that I'd be annoying you. Or something," I said.

"That's not your problem, dude! There's literally no way for you to know that. And guess what? I'm not a mind reader either!"

I... Huh. Hm.

Maybe she had a point. I was a friendless weirdo, but did that exclude me from having free will? I was allowed to talk or hang out with or avoid whoever I wanted just as much as anyone else. What I wasn't allowed to do was assume how those people would feel about it. Only they could decide that.

"So basically," I said, "I *am* allowed to talk to you?"

"At appropriate times and places!" That went without saying. I felt my lips start to turn up on their own. "What's that about? Stop that. It's weird."

"Nothing. Just, thank you. Really."

"I'll never understand you." Yanami sighed and shook her head. "Anyway, both of you! Don't forget what I said! Got it?"

"Yes, ma'am!" Hakamada and I replied together. Our hearts were one in that moment.

"Now, Sousuke," Yanami continued. "Apologize to Nukumizu-kun."

Wait, why?

Hakamada turned and bowed to me. "I'm sorry for getting you caught up in all this, Nukumizu."

I waved my hands and did the whole "oh, no, please" song and dance. To what end, I did not know.

"Nukumizu-kun, now you apologize to me," Yanami said.

"Um, okay?" I didn't question it. Questions would not help. "I'm sorry. I won't run my mouth anymore."

Yanami crossed her arms and nodded. "Good. I forgive you." She tilted her head next. "So, what now?"

No one knew. We all exchanged glances, and then the bell rang. Lunch break was over.

Yanami wiped a few remaining tears hanging from her eyelashes and smiled. "All right, whatever. Back to class, everyone.

About-face!" We about-faced. Yanami passed between us, slapping each of us on the back, and ran ahead. She turned and waved. "Don't be late, slowpokes!"

Hakamada put a hand on my shoulder. "Let's go," he said to me.

"R-right," I said back.

We looked at each other, wearing the same exhaustion on our faces, then followed after her.

***

The next day was the last of the semester.

Amanatsu-sensei stood at the podium at the front of the class and raised her voice above the clamor of antsy first-years itching to start their vacation. "Everyone come up in *seating order*! Seating order, kids!"

Because any other order and her brain would short-circuit trying to place names to the faces of her own students.

I picked up my report card and opened it up. Not bad for my first high school semester. What concerned me more was the comments section.

"Very passionate and driven committee member," it read.

Whoever that was, it wasn't me, and I didn't envy the someone who would have to show their parents the report card that read, "Has no friends. How are things at home?"

I plopped my chin in my hand and watched the rest of the class trip over themselves to compare grades. Yakishio, surprisingly not one of them, was face-down on her desk, clutching her head. Didn't envy her either.

"Dang, not bad," Hakamada said. He'd come over to sneak a peek at my card. "So Japanese and math are your specialties, huh?"

"I guess. Kinda whatever at the rest."

"Math's what got me. Summer school. Man, I so don't wanna come to campus on vacation."

"You don't have any clubs?" That earned a couple of points with me.

"Nah, can't join any. I do rock climbing on my own time."

Points: revoked. What maniac went out of their way to do extracurriculars *outside* of school? Just like that, all the goodwill we'd built came crashing down.

"Hit me up sometime. We should do karaoke," he said, heading back to Himemiya's desk.

He was good. Knew just the right amount of courtesy to make it impossible to hate him. No wonder they called people like him social *butterflies*. Granted, he very much lacked the grace.

My eyes wandered to Yanami. She and her friends were arguing over who had to share what grades for which subjects. Same old Yanami.

"All right, all right," Amanatsu-sensei called out when the buzz was beginning to die. "The sooner you get settled, the sooner summer break can start."

That put out the last of the lingering conversations. She waited for everyone to get back to their seats.

"Now, a word before you go scampering off." She coughed with as much effect as her tiny presence could muster. Wasn't often she tried to genuinely act serious. "However you choose to spend the next forty days, I ask that you do it with purpose. They'll fly before you know it, and all of a sudden it'll have been two years and you're up to your ears in college entrance exams."

For once, she was making some sense. The class waited for her to continue with bated breath.

Her tone dropped. "I hear you thinking to yourselves, 'Oh, it must be so nice being a teacher and getting all that time off.'" She slammed her fist into the podium. The impact said more than words could. "Well you'd be *wrong*! We are service workers! We don't *get* time off! Who do you think teaches summer school? Sets up classes for the interns? Prepares the new lesson plans? Attends the meetings? The study halls? Chaperones the club trips? Manages the paperwork?" Still deeper silence gripped the classroom. "Watch me make my friggin' VTuber debut next semester. I'm gonna wreck your data plans!" I made a mental note to look into flip phones. "Do you people even know how it feels to take one measly day off for Obon, only to be ostracized for it?! And before you say, 'Oh, just take it at a different time of year,' what do you think holidays are *for*?! Any other day, and now you're public enemy number one for having the *nerve* to make more work for your coworkers!"

She was losing the plot real fast. We had no business hearing any of this.

"Point being, be on your best behavior! I've got a lot riding on a class reunion this Obon, so don't you go acting a fool or getting so squirrelly that I have to waste my PTO cleaning your mess! Legs *shut*!"

What was even happening right now? We were just a bunch of poor teenagers, at the mercy of this tiny woman's rage. The silence hung heavier with every ragged breath she took.

When she was done panting, Amanatsu-sensei thwacked her attendance roster against the podium. "Anyway. Consider all that a bit of advice from your friendly neighborhood senpai. Now go on! You're on summer break now!"

***

The semester was officially over. I checked my watch. Just before noon.

I'd escaped the chaos of the classroom and come to the usual fire escape at the old annex. Summer clouds drifted overhead. The fields were empty, even the sports clubs taking a little respite from their practice. I played with a milk box in my hands. Force of habit had me grab one from a vending machine on the way here.

What now?

My Twin Sister Left to Be an Adventurer, Then Came Back a Demon Gyaru had just come out with a new volume. Maybe I'd grab that, then spend some alone time at the family restaurant.

"O-oh. You're here." Komari dropped her bag with a thud. I expected her this time. It was too nice a day out not to make use of it.

"Not going home?" I asked.

"K-killing some time first." She produced a roll—leftover from yesterday, no doubt.

I handed her my milk. "Here. Haven't had any."

"Y-you don't have to..." Desire twinkled in her eyes. "I-is that... the extra rich kind? Isn't that ten yen extra?"

This stray knew her stuff.

"Splurged a little. It's the last day of school."

"O-okay, but I still feel bad." She offered a handful of one- and ten-yen coins.

"Don't need any of that. Just take it."

"But th-that guy took your money yesterday, didn't he?"

"I was not mugged," I said.

"Th-then what *did* he take?" Desire twinkled in her eyes. Again. She would find no material here.

"Neither my heart nor my chastity, so chill."

That might have been half a lie. At least in regards to my heart.

Komari caught my moment of weakness and snatched it. She smiled up at me in a way I didn't think she could. "I knew s-something was going on! Wh-when did it start? I want all the details!" Her eyes sparkled. Her cheeks took on a rosy tint. Why was she being cute all of a sudden? And why was *this* what triggered it?

"There's no 'it,' so I've got nothing to tell. Eat your bread."

She made a nasty giggle. "Wh-why eat food when I'm already e-eating this up?"

I shouldn't have given her any fuel whatsoever. I considered sending her over to Tsukinoki-senpai so she could straighten her out, but my gut told me she'd do anything *but*.

"Wow, I've never been here before!" A bright and somewhat head-empty voice came from below. "The breeze is so nice." Yakishio ascended the stairs, saw us, and then whipped back around. "B-bad news, Yana-chan! I think they're having a moment!"

A moment of what? I thought sarcastically. But not for long. I was more interested in the name she'd called.

"Eh, it's Nukumizu-kun. What could we possibly be interrupting?" she said (quite rudely).

"Yanami-san?" I said as she came up. "Why are you here?"

"Do I need a reason? I'm the one who found this place first." Yanami stepped onto the landing. Her pout quickly changed to a leer. "Unless we *were* interrupting."

"Yeah, right. I'm the third wheel if anything."

"Hey now, us lonely singles gotta stick together," she teased.

Yakishio looked between us, then lit up. "Ohmigosh, Nukkun, you too? It's totally spreading! Is it happening?!"

She picked the weirdest things to get all hyper about. As someone else might say, that was her problem right there.

"So why'd you guys come over here anyway?" I asked. "Like, actually."

"I had a bit of time before I met up with the track team, so I was having Yana-chan show me to her super-secret base," Yakishio said, leaning concerningly far off the railing.

Yanami stood next to me. Not too close, not too far. An awkward middle. "Hey, does the lit club do anything over the summer?"

"Uhhh, not sure," I said. "Tsukinoki-senpai mentioned maybe getting together sometime."

Yakishio balanced her stomach against the rail so her feet floated off the ground and stuck her arms out. "Definitely lemme know! We could maybe go cicada hunting. That's summery."

More like noisy.

What kind of literature club was this? We'd just gotten back from an overnight beach trip and they already wanted more.

Extroverts. Sitting in a dark room typing out manuscripts sounded more fitting for a lit club to me.

Yanami watched Yakishio's legs flail and took a half step closer to me. "Hey, so, the trip was fun, yeah? Looking forward to the next one."

"If people are even comfortable with me around anymore now that Tsukinoki-senpai and the only other guy are an item," I said.

"Oh, for the love of..." She rolled her eyes. "The trip was fun because we *all* went. That includes you, doofus."

I looked away and to the side. "Well, yeah I...I guess. But hey."

"Hm?"

"It's nothing, just... Never mind. Forget it. I'll tell you later."

Komari eyed us closely. She and I shared a short moment, then she tugged at Yakishio's shirt.

"What's up?" Yakishio asked.

Komari instinctively reached for her phone. "U-um..." But she quickly put it back, hanging her head. "I was a l-little interested in running. I wanted to ask if you could t-teach me. Form and stuff."

Yakishio's eyes went wide as saucers. She grinned even wider and took her hand. "You bet I can!" she cried out. Komari meeped in response. "We'll get your hundred-meter below twelve seconds in no time!"

"I-I was actually thinking more long-distance?"

"Don't you worry! I've thought it all through! I call it the Yakishio Method!"

"The...Yakishio Method?" Komari's cheek twitched nervously. That didn't sound good.

"The idea's that long distance is really just a bunch of sprints back-to-back! If you can run a hundred meters, you just have to do that fifteen times and that's fifteen-hundred right there! Still working out the kinks, though."

"C-can we maybe start with something easy? Like, ph-physical rehab level."

"Okay, so the Yakishio Method Part Two. In that one, I'm working on proving that 1,500 meters will feel like a hundred if you literally just run for a full day nonstop. Let's get you on the track!"

Yakishio hauled Komari off, who whispered upon passing me, "You owe me."

She deserved a full liter of milk for that gambit.

Yanami watched them disappear down the stairs. "They're such good friends."

I didn't argue. "They sure are."

"It's weird," Yanami muttered.

"What is?"

She rested her elbows against the railing and looked at me. "I mean, think about it. I hardly knew who you or Komari-chan were not too long ago. I didn't even know what club you guys were in until we went on that trip." And yet she still came. "Writing's actually pretty fun. I even picked up some books Komari-chan recommended me, and I liked those too. Made me realize how cool stories can be."

Yanami gazed out at the students scurrying around campus, a little somberly. How nice that the written word could have such a profound and positive impact on—

"It's so easy to forget all the hard crap in life when you're reading. Nothing ever goes wrong for you on the page."

Correction: not so positive.

"Um. Take care of your mental health, Yanami-san," I said. "Maybe you can practice asceticism or fasting this summer."

She held her hands up and waved them in fervent denial. "Hey, I'm not *that* far gone! And you can forget fasting. So don't suggest it again. Ever."

Ah, there she was. That was the Yanami I knew. I'd been somewhat worried that the Hakamada thing yesterday would leave things weird, but no. Far from it.

Now was my chance.

Yanami blinked at me. "Whatcha starin' at?"

I put my hand to my chest and took a deep breath. "Yanami-san. I have something to ask you."

"Huh," she lazily replied. She blinked a few more times, then shot straight up. "Huh?! Wait, like, now?! Here?!"

"I don't know when we'll next have a moment to ourselves, so yeah."

She fussed and messed with her hair. "Wh-what if we gave it a bit?! Think about this, Nukumizu-kun! There's a time and place for—"

"I've done my thinking. And if I don't say it here, now, I know I'll regret it."

Yanami flattened her hair, straightened her collar, adjusted her ribbons, flattened her skirt, and faced me. Seemed I'd gotten through to her.

She made a cute little cough. "W-well, uh, go on. I'll hear you out. No promises, though."

I took a deep breath and met her gaze directly. The nerves were on their way.

"Yanami-san. Will you..."

"Will I?" she parroted.

My throat closed up. I forced it back open, and with every ounce of courage I could muster, I took a step forward. She jumped.

"Will you be my friend?!"

"I'm sorry I'd rather just be frie—"

We spoke over each other.

And then crushing silence.

A bird flapped its wings, perching onto the rail. It chirped a sad song.

When she had finally recovered from her petrification, Yanami's head fell to one side. "Your friend?"

I nodded. "Yes."

Yanami put her arms on the railing and let out a big, heavy, and long sigh. "Oh," she said, quieter than the bird's wings as it took off.

Were we not on the same page? Something told me she needed a little more context.

"Because, like, you've already paid back all the money," I explained. "So we can't have lunch together anymore. I mean, okay, we're classmates and clubmates, but if we're, um, friends, if you say yes, then we can still..." I stopped rambling and making wild hand gestures. "Wait. Hold on."

"I have been, thanks."

"Did you just...reject me? Without even a confession?"

"Sure seems that way, bud." She patted me on the shoulder. "Welcome to Losersville."

"But how can I have lost at something I wasn't even attempting? You're the one who made it a whole big thing."

Yanami's jaw dropped. "Okay, no! You can *not* blame me for that! I'm not crazy for expecting what I expected, so the rejection still counts!"

"Relax, Yanami-san. You clearly don't understand what an actual confession is."

"Are you seriously Nukumizu-splaining romance to me?"

Technically, she was 0–1, and I was 0–0. Statistically speaking, I had authority on matters of love.

"First of all, there needs to be at least a two-to-three-year friendship already in place. That's the stage where you get to know each other and figure out if you're compatible. Then, and only then, do you seal the deal at a place of great emotional significance for the two of you."

"You just described a proposal." This was fair. "Wait, does that mean you're proposing to me in three years? Should I go ahead and reject that ahead of time while I'm at it?"

"No. Do not pencil that into your calendar." I couldn't get anywhere with this girl. Relatedly, we'd almost bantered our way around the most important thing here. "Anyway, uh..."

"What?"

"Th-the friend thing." My voice died partway through speaking. "Where are we with that?"

"There you go getting all mumbly again. Yes, we're friends. We have been."

"Wait, we have?"

"What the heck else would you call us?" Yanami put her elbows back on the railing and turned her head to me, a goofy grin on her lips.

"Why're you looking at me like that?"

"That's what gets me about you. That right there."

"That right where?"

She didn't answer. Only giggled.

I made my best attempt at a crooked smile to return hers with.

I didn't regret the way I'd lived up to then. There was nothing wrong with being a loner. We all interacted with society and the people in it in our own ways.

There at our usual spot, though, I'd be lying if I said I disliked her company.

"Thank you, Yanami-san."

The words came from my heart.

Yanami saw the smile on my face, not so crooked anymore, and reacted in surprise. She did smile back, though.

"You're welcome." She held her fist out. "To rejection, fellow loser."

I bumped it, laughing. "Didn't lose squat."

Afterword

Hey there. I'm Takibi Amamori, this year's recipient of the Gagaga Award in the 15th annual Shogakukan Light Novel Awards. I am going to take the liberty of assuming that, because you have this book, you too are a gentleman/woman of taste with an appreciation for those heroines of a losing aspect.

The tears they shed, the heartbreak they suffer, the strength with which they face overwhelming odds, and the grace they flourish when the one they love chooses another—this is the losing heroine, and they embody everything there is to love about rom-coms. Through this novel, it is my sincerest hope that you see in losers the things that I do.

I am now going to invoke debut privileges so I can thank people at length.

Firstly, all those involved in the award selection process. I certainly wouldn't be writing this if not for you. Guest judge Carlo Zen-sensei, your constructive criticism in particular was invaluable to me during the editing process. I am extremely grateful.

Imigimuru-sensei, you brought life to the characters. Nukumizu, Yanami, and the rest of the gang owe their beautiful and picturesque world to you, and I can't properly put into words how it feels to see them in it. Thank you.

To all involved in the marketing and the otherwise behind-the-scenes work, and even the many bookstore employees, I thank you for getting my book into people's hands. It wouldn't have made it there without you.

I-senpai and Mr. D, your initial comments on the intro when I had barely started are what helped shape and guide this story to its final destination.

T-senpai, Mr. N, and Mr. W. A first draft is just that, only a first, and without your patient and thorough read-throughs, that destination might have been something else entirely.

When my work first came out online, I received so much invaluable feedback from so many readers. Your words have helped further me on my journey as a writer, and I hope we can continue to walk on it hand-in-hand.

To my editor, Mr. Iwaasa, words do no justice. Your patience for this oh-so green and sluggish author truly knows no bounds. Looking back, I can clearly see the picture that was put together, piece by piece, during this entire process. It was genuinely enlightening to see the transformation from draft to final product. I know there's still much I have to learn about the professional industry, and I'm confident the experience and skills you gave me will be ones that I continue to exercise for some time.

Lastly, I'd like to dedicate this book to my father, who let me bum around, unemployed, long before I had so much as a single toe on the ground in the author world. Thanks, Dad.

ABOUT THE AUTHOR
Takibi Amamori

Raised in Toyohashi, got a bit lost in Kanazawa, now living out the rest of my life in a corner of Kyushu. Not a heroine, yet somehow always losing.